# Beyond the Rain

## Aurora Melthin

Copyright © 2024 by Aurora Melthin

All rights reserved.

No portion of this book may be reproduced in any form without written permission from the publisher or author, except as permitted by U.S. copyright law.

# Contents

1. Chapter 1 — 1
2. Chapter 2 — 7
3. Chapter 3 — 13
4. Chapter 4 — 18
5. Chapter 5 — 23
6. Chapter 6 — 29
7. Chapter 7 — 35
8. Chapter 8 — 41
9. Chapter 9 — 47
10. Chapter 10 — 54
11. Chapter 11 — 59
12. Chapter 12 — 69
13. Chapter 13 — 77
14. Chapter 14 — 83
15. Chapter 15 — 90
16. Chapter 16 — 95
17. Chapter 17 — 102

| | |
|---|---|
| 18. Chapter 18 | 108 |
| 19. Chapter 19 | 113 |
| 20. Chapter 20 | 119 |
| 21. Chapter 21 | 125 |
| 22. Chapter 22 | 129 |
| 23. Chapter 23 | 135 |
| 24. Chapter 24 | 141 |
| 25. Chapter 25 | 148 |
| 26. Chapter 26 | 154 |
| 27. Chapter 27 | 160 |
| 28. Chapter 28 | 165 |
| 29. Chapter 29 | 171 |
| 30. Chapter 30 | 178 |
| 31. Chapter 31 | 183 |
| 32. Chapter 32 | 188 |
| 33. Chapter 33 | 194 |
| 34. Epilogue | 200 |

# Chapter 1

♥

X ylah sailor summer

"xylah. xylah." i heard repeatedly from the twins.

i only stared at them,"can you take us to the store?" kamari asked.

"no." i said pulling my cover over me and went back to my book before jamari snatched it from my hands.

"get the fuck out my room." i snapped at him as he frowned.

"pleaseee they gone and we want snacks." kamari said and i smacked my lips grabbing my card.

"doordash, $30 max." i said handing it to them.

they quickly ran out my room closing the door behind them, i pushed my glasses up my face before grabbing my book from the floor.

i wished for a little brother and got two spawned from hell.

i heard a loud snort and i looked over at my miniature pig,"you finally up..." i mumbled as she stood up from her bed.

most the time she was solo by herself chilling or in the backyard, every now and then she'd snuggle with me.

she went over to her small bowl of food and water as i placed a bookmark in my book 'of mice and men' and sat it down.

"thank you." jamari said comin back in my room and handed my card back.

"sorry for snatching your book.." he added.

"it's coo." i said and he went back out my room.

i placed my card back into my phone case making me check my phone.

ma: you up baby?ma: the twins haven't drove you wild yet?

-they ordered snacks wit my card

ma: that pantry full of snacks

-yk yo kids fat asf

ma laughed at 'yk yo kids fat asf'

ma: xylah them yo brothers

-they yo offspring

namari: you gonna come to my show tonigh?

-the gallery?

namari: yeah, if youn want youn have to

-i'll come what time will it be?

namari: 8, you don't have to stay the whole time

-okay i'll come and i'll ride wit you

namari loved 'okay i'll come and ride wit you'

namari: alr i love you

-i love you too

i put my phone down and went to my connected bathroom, i put my passion twists up in a high bun then turned on my shower.

i stared into the mirror as i started undressing myself, i was definitely gonna have my mothers body. it was a blessing and a curse all at once.

i'm 16 about to be 17, but everyone felt i was older because my body developed a tad bit faster than normal i guess.

i started getting into makeup last year and you could've swore i told namari i was pregnant the way she reacted. she chased me around with makeup wipes for about 2 hours straight.

but i didn't wear much makeup usually still looking natural, and i only wore lash strips.

i took a shower then got out and wrapped my robe around me, i moisturized my body and my face before spraying some vanilla perfume on.

i walked to my closet and tried to decide on what to wear, i was only going to the library then probably starbucks.

i grabbed a blue nike hoodie, grey biker shorts, and grey slides.

i put that on then put on my pandora charm bracelet, namari bought it when i was younger and over the years she'd buy charms to fill it up.

i grabbed my headphones and placed them around my neck.

i heard the front door open letting me know ma was home, i grabbed my phone and keys before walking out my room.

"ma, i'm finna go to the library." i said once i saw her in the living room.

"okay baby, be safe love you." she said kissing my cheek.

"love you too."

"hey xylah, are you looking for anythin specific?" the librarian, mrs cherry, asked.

"no ma'am, just looking.." i said quietly and she nodded goin back to organizing books.

i walked down different isles and looked at the books spines to see if anything would catch my eye.

i adjusted the setting on my headphones to noise canceling, i went to my phone and clicked on charlene by anthony hamilton.

i finally found a book i was interested in 'what if it's us' the title read.

i grabbed it then went to sit at one of the tables that was more isolated.

i sat down and opened up and book being careful to not break the spine, it was a fairly new book still.

as i read i also made sure to check my surroundings since i couldn't clearly hear much going on around me.

i went to check my phone and i quietly laughed seeing the twins had text me.

kamari: where'd you go

jamari: and why you ain't tell us you was leaving

-y'all not my parents

kamari: that's not the point

-library

jamari: all you had to say

i put my phone back up and went back to my book until i felt a tap on my shoulder, i slowly turned around.

i almost had to break my neck to look up at him, he was tall as shit.

i pulled down my headphones as he started "i'm s-sorry if i'm bothering you..." he said before clearing his throat to speak again.

"i've seen you a f-few times here before..i was wondering if i could get y-your number.." he said and i noticed his cheeks were lightly red.

mmm cute.

i nodded my head as i held my hand out for his phone, he placed it in my hand and i put in my number and name.

"xylah?" he pronounced correctly making me nod.

"my name is azaire." he said without stuttering.

"i'll text y-you later.." he said getting ready to walk off before i spoke.

"hey?" i called out quietly and he looked at me.

"do you like starbucks?" i asked before looking down at the book i was reading placing a bookmark in it.

i laughed quietly as he eyed the drink,"just try it." i said and he shook it around some before speaking.

"your voice is s-soft and pretty." he said making my face heat up.

he finally took a sip of the drink and scrunched up his face,"what?" i asked as i finished my iced white mocha with sweet foam.

"ion know...it's a-actually good." he said taking another sip. i ordered him an iced caramel macchiato with extra caramel and sweet foam on top.

"so...how old are you?" i asked.

"17."

i scrunched up my face,"really? you look 19..." i said and he shrugged.

"you look...ion k-know maybe 18." he said and i shook my head.

"i'm 16, i turn 17 soon tho." i said and he nodded.

"so you thought i was older than you?"

"i wouldn't h-have cared to be honest..i mean i already graduated." he said and i raised my eyebrows.

"oh....so you're smart?" i asked and he laughed.

"sumn like that.." he said and i nodded.

so shorter sentences he doesn't stutter as much.

"are you gonna go to college?" i asked and he shrugged.

"m-might just do a gap year...a-and work for my dad."

"mm okay...soo what you do in your free time?"

this might have be the most i've talked in a while. not that i was complaining, his voice was satisfying to listen to even with his stutter.

it was kinda cute....

"work, spend time wit f-friends, or i'm playing basketball...what about you?"

"i'm most likely reading or with my family..." i said and he nodded before finishing his drink.

i looked down at my phone seeing it was getting late,"hey i'm sorry to cut this short...i need to get home tho.." i said and he nodded.

"it's f-fine...i'll text you.." he said as we both got up.

"yeah...i enjoyed this though." i said and he smiled making me smile.

get a grip xylah!

i finally left and got in my car and placed my head on the steering wheel, thinking about him gave me a weird fuzzy feeling inside.

oh god...i'm getting roaches- wait it's butterflies.

# Chapter 2

♥

**X**ylah sailor summer

i sat at my vanity and stared at my appearance, i had on light makeup and just finished any touch ups on it.

i looked over in the corner of my room and saw my miniature pig was asleep and staring at my ipad that i had playing blues clues.

what? that's my child foreal.

i focused back in the mirror before quickly doing my lip combo and fixed my edges, i heard my phone go off making me check it.

unknown: this azaire

i smiled before saving his number.

azaire: this azaire

-heyy

azaire: wyd

-gettin ready to go with my parents

azaire: igh, text me when you not busy

you liked 'igh, text me when you not busy'

-i will, it might be late tho

azaire: that's fine, i should be up

"xylah!" i heard from outside my door.

"come in mama." i said and she opened my door before pouting.

"aweee my baby looks so prettyyyy." she dragged out and i quietly laughed as i stood up and gave her a quick hug.

"thank you, you look good too ma...already know namari ain't letting you out her sight." i said and she laughed.

"i'm glad you like this dress..." she said adjusting the black dress i had on.

it was off the shoulders and came a lil below mid-thigh, and i wore nude sandals on my feet.

i started messing with the bracelet on my wrist,"mama you got my earbuds yet?" i asked and she nodded.

"they were in the mailbox when i got home, i'll give them to you before we leave."

"okay i'll just wear them to some places...i get weird looks when i have on my headphones a lot." i mumbled.

"girl fuck them people." she said and i shook my head before grabbing my phone.

"are the twins coming?" i asked and she shook her head no.

"they're actually staying the night with nalani, she's gonna take them to school in the morning." she said and i nodded.

"so how was the library?" she asked and i pointed to the book on my bed.

"i checked that one out today...and made a friend..." i said and she raised her eyebrow at me.

"a friend? what's her name?" she asked and i chewed on my lip.

"uhh..his name..." i started off and her eyes widened.

"you gotta boyfriend?!" she said and i quickly shushed her.

i don't know how close namari is to my room.

"my bad-"

"ma no, he came up to me at the library and i gave him my number." i said and she smirked.

"what he look like?"

"ion got a picture of him, he cute tho." i said and she nodded.

"you growing tooo damn much girl." she laughed before walking out my room.

i walked around the art gallery and admired all the different paintings and styles hanging on the wall.

people were quietly whispering among themselves, i spotted namari and walked over to her.

"you ight?" she asked putting her arm over my shoulder and pecked my forehead.

"yeah...all these paintings are nice. when are you going to present yours?" i asked and she looked at her apple watch.

"about 5 minutes...you had fun at the library?" she asked and i nodded my head.

"anything interesting happen?"

i know DAMN well....

"not really..." i mumbled looking away from her.

"i'm still hurt you didn't bring me no starbucks back." she said and i laughed.

"closed mouth don't get fed..." i shrugged and she shook her head.

"yeah yeah go find ya mama, i gotta get ready." she said before walking off.

it didn't take long for me to find mama, it's easy for me to find her anywhere.

"your lil friend text you?" she asked and i smacked my lips.

"mama." i simply said and she laughed.

"my bad my bad...lemme find out my baby gotta crush." she said before giving her attention to namari who was now on the mic.

i sighed as i changed out the dress into a big t-shirt and boy shorts.

i used makeup wipes for my face then put my bonnet on, i got comfortable in my bed and placed my phone on charge.

-you still up?

azaire: yea

-wydd?

azaire: smokin

-this late??

azaire: yeah my mama cookin, food taste better when i'm high

-oh ok

azaire: wyd

-laying down, just got back home not too long ago

azaire: what y'all went to do

-art gallery, my mom paints

azaire: that's wassup

-yeah i was just texting you

azaire: ight pretty you have a goodnight

- you too

azaire loved 'you too'

i put my phone down and grabbed the book what if it's us and started back reading.

not gonna lie the book was good so far, but at the same time i was a sucker for any books that had any kind of progressing romance.

once i got half way thru the book i stopped reading and sat my glasses down on my nightstand. i grabbed my ipad and turned on a random movie.

i propped my ipad up on my night stand and pulled the cover up to my neck and focused on haunted house.

my phone went off making me grab it.

azaire: ik i told you have a good night, but you still up?

-yeah, you ok?

azaire: yeah i'm just bored

-weren't you smoking?

azaire: i was, just got done eating

-ohh what about your friends?

azaire: they all doing they own shit rn

-i mean....if you want you can ft me

not even 5 seconds later.

i shook my head and answered on my ipad,"hey." i said once the call connected.

his eyes were low and he had on a white tank top with a durag on his head,"you k-know you look good bare face..." he said and i shrugged.

"i mean im ight." i said and he chuckled lightly.

"what you doing still up?"

"i wasss watching a movie before you called." i said and he nodded.

"what you watching?"

"hanuted house on disney plus...i was watching it on my ipad and you on that soo." i trailed off.

"share yo screen, i've n-never seen that before." he said.

"awe not you wanting to watch a movie wit me." i teased and watched him roll his eyes while his cheeks turned red.

i clicked on share screen and started the movie over since i was only a few minutes in,"and you better stay quiet while we watchi ng...we can have a mini discussion about the movie like every 30 minutes since it's 2 hours long." i explained.

  he laughed and nodded his head,"i hear you."

# *Chapter 3*

♥

Xylah sailor summer

    Gotta change my answering machineNow that I'm alone'Cause right now it says that we can't come to the phone

played quietly through my headphones as i finished crocheting the top of the two piece i was making.

i took an interest in crocheting a few months ago, at first just small patches and designs but then i decided to actually try and make clothes.

and so far it's been good.

once i finished the two piece i tried it on and was happy with how it turned out.

the skirt ended up being a tad bit shorter then i expected due to my hips and butt. i wasn't complaining much it still looked good.

the top made my titties sit up a bit more but nothing too crazy, i smiled at my appearance and pushed my passion twists to one side.

i took off my headphones then walked out my room and knocked on mama's door before slowly opening it.

she was currently installing a new wig,"yes my- oh my gosh you look so cute." she said as she tied a scarf around her edges.

"thank you- i jus finished making it." i said and she smiled at me.

"you did great, when you get time you should make me a lil dress." she said and i nodded.

"just send me a picture of one, i'll try to make sumn similar." i said.

"okay i will, and i was thinking later on we get our nails done and go out to eat." she said.

"yeah we can, what about the twins and namari?"

"they're gonna go do their own thing and meet us at the restaurant." she said.

"ohh okay." i said before walking back to my room, i heard snorting from outside my door making me open it again.

i laughed seeing mama must have put a pink tutu on her, i carefully picked her up and placed her on my lap once i sat on my bed.

"i gotta order you some more clothes..." i said as she started pushing her snout against my arm.

i grabbed my phone seeing azaire had text me.

azaire: wyd

-holding my pig

azaire: ???

-i have a miniature pig

then he started calling me, i answered the facetime and propped my phone up on my dresser.

"what the f-fuck?" he mumbled seeing her in my lap.

"what's the name?"

"her name is coco." i said and he nodded.

"why you never said you had- a pet pig?"

"cause it's not sumn i really brag about, but she's cute and i like her so." i said before sitting her back down on the ground.

she went over to her bed before plopping onto her side.

"you look p-pretty." he said and i felt my face heat up.

"oh! i actually made this myself...it took months." i said standing up and he nodded.

"it looks...short."

"it is." i said grabbing my phone laying it on the bed.

"what you doing today??" he asked as i undressed.

"later my mom and i are getting our nails done then i'm going out to eat." i said grabbing a black crop top then a pair of ripped jeans.

"oh...i was going to see if you w-wanted to go to starbucks real quick?" he mumbled and i noticed he seemed nervous to ask.

"yeah i can, i'll meet you there?" i asked.

"o-okay...in 10 minutes?" he asked and i nodded.

"yeah i'll be there."

"ight." he said before hanging up.

i put half my passion twists up in a ponytail and let the rest hang, i quickly did my edges then checked how my makeup looked.

i put on my white forces then grabbed my keys before letting my mom know where i was about to go.

"oh— tell your lil friend i said hi." she added as i walked out the room.

"the inside of your car niceee." i said as i got comfortable in the passenger seat.

he had a dark orange mustang, his seats and floor mats were matching the outside of the car while everything else was black

"preciate it.." he said before sipping on my very berry hibiscus refresher.

"just have it." i mumbled and he laughed.

"my b-bad, yo shit just taste better." he said and i took his drink.

i used a different straw and finished his vanilla frappe mixed with caramel drizzle.

"mmm...what you been doing today?" i asked looking over at him.

the driver seat leaned back and his legs were spread out, he had on a tan nike tech with matching sweats. on his feet white forces. this time he wasn't wearing a durag or beanie his waves on display.

"went to work, smoked wit my friends. now i'm wit you." he said.

"you?

"i did school work and finished the two piece, that's it really. a lil reading in between." i said and he nodded his head.

"you should c-come wit me one day." he said and i raised my eyebrow.

"what you- im sorry can you turn the ac down the sound bothering my ears..." i mumbled rubbing my ear.

i forgot my headphones.

he turned the ac down before speaking,"like meet my f-friends... only if you want tho. you don't h-have to right now."

"i can, it might do me some good actually...ion really hangout wit nobody besides my family and books." i shrugged.

"ight...they kinda wanna meet you." he said and i scrunched my face up.

"they- you be talking to them about me?" i asked with a smirk and he rolled his eyes looking off.

"nah they noticed i be o-on my phone more...and i just said i made a new f-friend." he said.

"mmm..speaking of my ma said to tell you hi."

"next time we on the p-phone lemme speak to her." he said and i pursed my lips together.

"ion know about allat now.." i mumbled making him laugh.

"oh lemme show you..i don't know which nail design i exactly want, i want them kinda long tho.." i said going to Pinterest.

"okay lean over here." i told him and he sat up and leaned over the console.

"so see...i like these...anddd these- oh and this one too." i said swiping between the three pictures.

"i think those are th-the best choice." he said swiping to the ones that were french tip with purple and glitter and a few matching charms.

"stop i was hoping you chose them too." i said making him lightly chuckle.

i looked up from my phone and noticed how close we actually were, he stared at me for a few seconds before moving back and clearing his throat.

he grabbed his phone and i could see 'dad' across the screen before he answered,"hello...i'm n-not at home...now?...."

he groaned dragging his hand down his face,"okay i'm coming..." he said before hanging up.

"i gotta go..i'm sorry." he said looking over at me.

"no it's okay, i should get going anyway...call me tonight?" i asked and he nodded.

"we gonna watch another movie?"

it kinda became a routine after the first night, i ended up falling asleep mid movie making us go to sleep on the phone since he was still on my ipad when i woke up.

"yeah, you can pick it tonight." i said as i started to get out the car.

"hollon...let's make a h-handshake.." he suggested.

# Chapter 4

♥

Azaire kade carmine

i got out my car and walked inside the trap,"yooo ain't seen yo ass in a minute ace!!" manman said as he dapped me up.

i nodded my head at him and continued to the main room in the house,"wassup son.." my dad said as i pushed the door open.

i stared at him and noticed a few other men in the room,"i need you to transfer some shit fa me...i'll get 5,000 in yo account by the morning." he said and i nodded

"so..where was you at before coming here?" he asked and i looked around at the other men in the room.

"aye, y'all get out real quick lemme talk to my son." he said making them leave.

i finally sat down beside him and sighed, whenever it came to this business i barely spoke around other muthafuckas unless it was serious.

mainly cause nobody would take someone with a stutter serious, they would just see it as fear or an advantage but it was neither.

"so..." my dad trailed off.

"was chillin wit someone..."

"someone? you done got a girlfriend or sumn?" he asked and i shook my head.

"nah...just b-been chillin wit her."

"so that's who you been on the phone wit lately? gigglin and shit." he said and i rolled my eyes.

"gigglin is a r-reach...you've talked to mama today?" i asked and he nodded.

"she gonna be getting off work soon..." he said checking his watch.

my mama was a nurse, did she have to work? absolutely not but she didn't like staying at home all week everyday she only worked 3 days out the week.

"ight...where the shit at??" i asked and he handed me a paper with an address and different numbers on it.

"now listen...imma get ya mama from work, be at the house before we get there." he said and i nodded.

my mama didn't know...i helped my dad wit all this. she found out when i started which was around 14 and my dad swore i wouldn't help anymore but...you see that was a lie.

i walked out the room and started my way out the trap when i found a hand grasp my arm making me snatch away,"damnn my bad...i was just tryna holla at you ace." macie said biting her lip.

this women been here for as long as i can remember it just kills me cause she 4 years older than me making her 21.

"macie! what i've told you about tryna fuck my son?" my dad asked with a glare.

"boy he is damn near grown." she said and i shook my head walking out the trap.

as i walked out i noticed an SUV driving past slowly making me raise my eyebrows before heading to my car.

-have people outside this car driving hella slow out here

dad: ok

i quickly left not wanting to get caught in any kind of shooting today, i've had enough of that already.

"AZAIRE!!!" i heard my mama voice making me roll out my bed and walk out my room to the living room.

"hey mama." i said smiling and hugged her.

"what you been doing??" she asked as i sat by her on the couch.

"earlier i was wit my f-friends, that's it really."

"mhmm...so who this girl you been talking to?"

i shook my head,"ma—"

"nah cause you must really like her, it's been a minute since i've known of you trying to talk to anyone besides your friends..." she said and i sighed.

she wasn't wrong.

"her name is xylah..." i said and she smiled.

"her name is pretty, you got a picture of her?" she asked and i nodded.

"it's a facetime photo, she was t-talking about her lil brothers spending all her m-money." i said pressing the photo of xylah that showed her in the kitchen with an oversized t-shirt and her passion twist up in a messy bun.

"ohhh she's beautiful baby." she said grabbing my phone and started swiping-

"okay." i said quickly grabbing my phone.

"also...you know you got a speech therapy appointment in the morning right??" she asked and my mood dropped immediately.

i've been going to them ever since i was 7, it helped a little i don't stutter with every word like i did at 7...but it still doesn't erase the trauma that caused me to start stuttering in the first place.

"and you need to go, i've let you miss out on the last two." she said and i nodded.

"imma go..." i mumbled getting up and walked back to my room.

i grabbed my phone and could see xylah calling me, i answered the facetime call and laughed seeing only her forehead and bonnet.

"move back girl." i said and she laughed moving back.

i took a photo of her making her smack her lips,"stop you always do that when i look a mess.." she mumbled.

"no i don't...lemme see y-your nails." i said and she flipped the camera.

her nails looked exactly like the picture i picked," i know you said you w-wanted them long...but that's long as hell." i said and she flipped the camera around.

"bad bitches have long nails...sometimes ion know cause shorties be cute too not gonna lie." she said and i nodded.

"my mama said you beautiful." i said and she raised her eyebrow.

"waittt you showed her one of them ugly facetime photos?"

"n-no...it was a facetime photo but you looked good." i said and she pursed her lips together.

"mmm okay...if you say so."

"xylah!!" i heard in the background.

"yes second madre." xylah replied putting the phone down.

"i put some money in yo account— who you on the phone wit?"

"namari— moveeee!" xylah laughed as she picked up her phone.

"is that a negro???"

"yes now thank you for the money-"

"lemme talk to him."

"nooo." xylah dragged out.

"why? he yo boyfriend? you like him??"

i laughed some before i was put on mute.

it was a few minutes before she took me off mute,"my bad." she said scratching her head.

"you good shawty." i said shaking my head.

"sooo what movie you wanna watch?" she asked.

"i know you said it was my turn to p-pick...but i think you should." i said and she sighed.

she sat up the phone and i could see she had on a white tank top with shorts.

she was swiping on her ipad i guess looking,"wanna watch a scary movie?" she asked looking over at the screen and i nodded my head.

"imma switch you to my ipad in a minute i gotta pee hollon." she said before getting up.

goddamn

i wasn't tryna stare but she got an ass on her- it fit her body perfectly.

i shook my head getting rid of any thoughts i shouldn't be thinking this early.

she came back and hung up before calling me back,"now you on my ipad, get comfy." she said and i laughed as she started sharing her screen.

# Chapter 5

♥

**Xylah sailor summer**

i groaned as i stretched and grabbed my phone to check the time.

3:46pm

my 30 minute nap ended up being 3 hours.

i looked around my room not seeing coco, she was most likely in the backyard.

i sat up and went to check my messages.

aunt nalani: whenever you get time call me girl, i miss talking to my niece.

-i'll call you in a few minutes i'm sorry.

uncle rome: why namari telling me about you talking to some nigga?? what's his name

-business!!!

uncle rome: lil girl you is my business.

namari: what's that boy name

-you can walk in my room

azaire: you up yet?azaire: i had to go wit my dad and do some shit wit him

-i'm up now

azaire: ik we ain't hung out in a lil minute, my friends gonna be doing sumn later you can come wit me if you want

-mmm when?

azaire: the next hour, even if you don't go i still wanna take you out somewhere

-take me out???

azaire: that's what i said xylah

-i can meet your friends tho

azaire: ight want me to pick you up?

-if you cool wit meeting my parents yeah

azaire: i will it's no problem

before i had time to digest the text my bedroom door opened and namari jumped on the bed beside me.

"who is he??" she asked glaring at me.

"fix yo face...his name azaire, i meet him at the library and he 17." i said and she nodded.

"he treat you right?"

"uhhh we don't date—"

"y'all went out before???"

"we've been to starbucks together anddd the library of course." i said and she nodded head once again.

"he hurt yo feelings, call me..i'll put his ass 6 feet under." she said getting off my bed.

"you not in that lifestyle no mo." i said and she pointed at me.

"stay in a child's place."

"anyways....he coming to pick me up." i said and her eyes widened.

"he— BABY!!" she yelled walking out my room and i winced rubbing my ear.

i shook my head before calling nalani,"hey grown butt." she said and i laughed holding the phone against my ear.

"hey aunt nalani." i said into the phone.

"you've been good?"

"yes ma'am, how you surviving wit the twins and koa?"

"chile i'm making it, them lil niggas know they can eat." she said and i laughed.

him meeting my parents actually went smooth, namari didn't go overboard like i thought and of course my mom was nice as hell.

now we were sitting outside an apartment complex as he answered his phone,"nigga i'm o-outside now, we coming..." he said getting out the car.

i did the same as he came over to my side mugging me,"what?" i asked and he reopened the door.

"get back in."

"why?" he didn't answer he just stared at me until i did.

he closed the door back then opened it again,"don't open doors when i'm around." he said as i got out.

i shook my head before adjusting my sea green pretty little thing bodysuit with the matching sweats.

i had took out my passion twists so my natural hair was slicked back into a bun with dramatic edges.

"you look pretty." he said making my face heat up.

"come on." he said making me follow behind him.

he had on tan essential shorts with a black tank top and black slides, he had in silver stud earrings and a matching silver chain around his neck.

i followed him before he knocked on a door,"yooo azaire!! wassup fuck nigga!!" a brown skinned said dapping azaire up.

i had in my earbuds so they weren't as noticeable, and they made everything sound more quiet then it actually was.

"wassup benz, this xylah." he said stepping aside so i could be seen.

"damn- shawty you fine as hell." benz said and azaire punched his shoulder.

"shit nigga my bad." benz mumbled holding his shoulder then let us in.

"you didn't have to hit him like that.." i said looking up at azaire.

he hummed in response before more people came into view,"oh shit- azaire you came just in time." a lightskin dude said holding a bottle of henny.

"sup taylin, i'm not even drinking today." azaire said as he sat on a separate couch pulling me beside him.

"more for me hell." taylin said opening the bottle.

i heard footsteps come from the hall,"hey azaire, this her?" a brown skin girl said walking in with another girl behind her.

azaire nodded his head taking out his phone.

"heyy i'm ayani, and this sage." ayani said then pointed to the girl beside her.

"hi i'm xylah."

"your name pretty." sage said making me smile.

"thanks." i said and she nodded before grabbing the bottle from taylin.

"you think just cause you my bitch you can do whatever you want." taylin said mugging her and she sat in his lap.

"that's exactly what i think the fuck." she said before drinkin some out the bottle.

"you drink or anything??" ayani asked making me shake my head no.

"oh shit my brownies!" sage said before getting up and i guess heading towards the kitchen.

"bitches probably burnt as fuck..." benz said shaking his head.

i could feel someone starin at me and i slightly turned my head meeting azaire's eyes.

"what??" i mumbled and he shook his head.

"you comfortable?" he asked and i nodded my head.

"so...how'd y'all meet?" benz asked sitting across from us.

"nigga leave them be." taylin said shaking his head.

"shit i just wanna know...cause when azaire be here he be all up in that phone smiling and shit." benz shrugged and azaire smacked his lips.

"fuck up....one of y'all g-gotta lighter??" azaire asked pulling out a gar pack from his pocket.

"hmm, and don't take my shit." taylin said handing him one.

"yo shit got yo girl on it..ion want it.." azaire mumbled and i looked closer at the lighter seeing sage's face was on it.

now that's cute.

"hollon...you want me to m-move??" azaire asked as he took out a rolled blunt from the pack.

"why?" i quickly asked looking at him.

to say i was attached to him was an understatement, maybe cause i don't usually talk to someone a lot or be around them much.

"you wanna be smelling like weed??"

"i got perfume you can use before you leave if you need to." ayani spoke up.

"okay thanks." i said and she nodded.

"imma scoot over a lil, ion wanna be blowing smoke in yo face." he said before scooting over and lit the blunt.

i watched as he inhaled the smoke before blowing it out, he did this a few more times before passing it to taylin.

"if the smell become too much lemme know." he told me and i nodded.

"i don't w-wanna get you high." he said making me nod again.

it's not like i haven't been high before, i just never really cared for it. it happened once when namari smoked but she forgot i was still in my mama room.

"damn y'all smoking already?" sage asked coming in with a plate that had brownies on it.

"and is." ayani said making me see she now had the blunt in her hand.

the blunt was passed around more before it got back to azaire, i tapped his thigh making him look at me.

"can i hit it?" i asked and he looked at me skeptically.

"one hit." he said holding it for me, i wrapped my lips around the end and inhaled before he pulled it back.

i inhaled the smoke before blowing it out, my throat burned for a few seconds before it went away.

"she ain't gonna feel nun off one hit." ayani said and azaire waved her off.

"she don't need to." he said taking a hit.

he was about to pass it before looking back at me,"mane here, you not finna b-be high as fuck on me.

i grabbed it from him and took two more hits before passing it,"yo ghosts clean as hell." benz said cheesing hard.

"he high as fuck." taylin said before laughing.

# *Chapter 6*

♥

**X**ylah sailor summer

"just keep yo eyes closed." azaire said as his car came to a stop.

i listened and heard his door open and close before mines opened, he helped me out the car before closing the door.

"okay, y-you facing me open your eyes." he said and i opened my eyes seeing his face then the bouquet of flowers towards me.

"you're giving me the money in here too??" i asked taking it from him.

he chuckled before nodding his head,"of course, now look where we at." he said and i turned around holding the flowers close to me.

i found myself smiling hard as i stared at the place in front of us, it was a cafe that opened not too long ago but it was also a library in a way.

"you remembered i wanted to come here..." i said looking back at him.

"y-yeah, you was excited as hell for i-it to open." he said and i opened his door and placed the flowers in the passenger seat then closed the door.

i followed closely beside him as we walked across the street to get to the cafe, he held the door open for me and i walked in first inhaling the mixture of coffee and pastries.

i walked up to the register and felt azaire close behind me, usually i'd want people away from me but him being close didn't bother me too much.

"can i get two small mocha lattes?" i asked the cashier and she nodded her head.

"it's gonna be $10.16." azaire handed me his card and i tapped it against the machine seeing approve pop up quickly.

we went to sit down and waited for our drinks,"you gonna look at some b-books while we here?" azaire asked making me nod my head.

"we can go to the second floor i wanna see what it all really looks like...but we should ask each other questions.." i said and he shrugged.

"go ahead."

"okay....what's your middle name and favorite color??" i asked him.

"kade, and i d-don't have a favorite color. now what's your middle name and what made you w-want a miniature pig?" he asked and i lightly laughed.

"sailor, and when i was younger my parents and i went to the bahamas where there were swimming pigs. and apparently i started getting attached to them then." i said and he nodded.

"sailor is pretty, i haven't heard that name much really." he said and i shrugged.

"you have any siblings??"

"nah o-only child...what you wanna do when you older?" he asked and i pursed my lips together.

"you can't judge me." i said holding out my pinky.

"i feel like yo ass g-gonna say stripper or sumn..." he mumbled linking his pinky wit mines.

"i wanna be a housewife." i said and he raised his eyebrows.

"really??" he asked making me nod.

"yes like i'd have my own money saved up buttt i'd really jus enjoy staying home making sure everything straight...like even when i have a baby i'd be a stay at home mom i don't care." i said truthfully and he nodded.

"what about you?" i asked and he seemed deep in thought for a second.

"honestly just run my own business so i could plan my own hours in a way." he said.

"wait don't you work right now??" i asked and he looked off before looking back at me.

"yeah."

"where you work at?" i asked and he cleared his throat.

"my dad—"

"2 mocha lattes!!" i noticed he let out a breath and got up to grab our lattes.

"upstairs??" he asked walking back to the table.

i grabbed mines and nodded my head walking ahead of him.

i made it up the stairs and was surrounded by different bookshelves,"i'll find a book for us, you f-find somewhere to sit.." he said.

"i wanna stay by you..." i mumbled.

"come on then." he said

i followed him around before he picked out a book we agreed on, he followed me and i pointed at a bean bag that was in the corner by a window.

i sat our drinks on the window sill and he sat down on the bag making it sink, i laughed a lil before sitting in between his legs.

i wasn't too close up on him, but we were close,"hmm hold the book..." i said as he carefully reached around me to open the book.

we spent almost 2 hours reading and talking before walking back to his car, it was starting to get dark.

"so...d-did you enjoy today??" he asked as he drove.

"yeah...i did actually thanks.." i said grabbing his free hand and started playing with his fingers.

he laughed some making me look at him,"what?" i asked and he shook his head.

"your tattoos are cool..." i mumbled staring at the ink on his hand.

"preciate it.." he said and i pursed my lips together in thought.

"can we get some chic fil a? i'll buy it im jus a lil hungry." i asked.

"i'll pay ma, i was g-getting hungry too." he said and i nodded feeling my face heat up.

"can i tell you sumn?" i asked and he nodded stopping at a red light then looked over at me.

"i really like...being around you and talking to you, it's all kinda new to me..." i said looking away from his eyes.

he started back driving when the light turned green,"i like yo presence, not gonna lie it c-calms me down sometimes." he said.

"it's sumn more you should know tho." i said and he glanced at me before looking back at the road.

"so like....i'm autistic and this is really like my first experience with a boy." i admitted and i felt my cheeks flush with embarrassment.

"okay...that's fine with me, i d-don't look at you differently." he shrugged.

"really??" i asked surprised and he nodded turning into chic fil a's parking lot.

"i mean you have to deal w-with my stutter..i'm sure it gets annoying." he said and i pouted a lil.

"no...i don't mind it's kinda cute." i said and he laughed.

"cute? yeah okay." he said shaking his head.

"i'm foreal...i think i like you." i said and he looked over at me with a different look on his face.

"i like you too..." he said before rolling his window down.

first he ordered his meal then mines, he paid and we got our food pretty fast.

i smiled grabbing my milkshake and immediately started drinking it,"thank you for everything again.." i said as he started driving again.

he nodded his head and drove with one hand while eating with the other.

we finished our food in a comfortable silence just as he pulled up to my house.

"umm i'll throw this away..." i mumbled gathering my trash.

"nah i got it, lemme w-walk you to the door tho." he said getting out.

he walked over and opened the door for me then shut it back once i was out.

"i'm hoping...you'll let me take you out a-again." he said as we walked up the few steps to the door.

"yeah, definitely it was fun...and your friends seem cool." i said making him laugh.

"you'll warm up to their w-weird asses." he said and i nodded.

"it's okay if i hug you?" he asked and i smiled opening my arms.

i wrapped my arms around his torso and he carefully hugged me, i inhaled his scent smelling weed and cologne mixed.

i pulled back not being entirely use to this yet,"wait! i forgot my flowers." i said and he chuckled.

"imma get it for you s-stay right here." he said and jogged back to his car.

the door opened revealing namari,"damn y'all was just standing out here." she said and i felt her finger move around my neck making me smack her hand away.

"i'm tryna make sure yo ass ain't got no hickeys." she said and i shook my head as azaire walked back to me and handed the flowers over.

"oh- you got MONEY." namari said grabbing the bouquet.

"i'll call you later." i told azaire and he nodded laughing and walked back to his car.

"you embarrassing..." i mumbled walking in the house behind her.

"anyways- BAE! yo daughter got taste. this nigga got money in the damn bouquet." she yelled going down the hall.

# Chapter 7

♥

## Azaire kade carmine

i clenched my jaw as my mama poured alcohol on my wound,"shit hurt huh?" she asked and i could tell she was mad so i stayed quiet.

i looked over at my dad who was leaning on the door frame with an unreadable expression on his face.

"so y'all gonna tell the truth about what happened??" she asked as she started putting stitches in my arm.

"mama-"

"son...don't." dad said and i sighed knowing he was just going to try and lie me out of this.

"nah i'm not stupid aaron, you still got him doing street shit?" she asked looking over at him pausing on my stitches.

"man no it ain't nun like that, we was just at the wrong place at the wrong time..." he said and she rolled her eyes before she started back stitching me up.

the pain medicine was starting to wear off and i started to feel the needle going in and out of my skin, it wasn't like this was my first rodeo but it still hurt like shit.

"i'm done...make sure you change the bandage and clean the area before you go to sleep and when you wake up..." she said standing up and walked past my dad.

"man marie-"

"i don't wanna hear it aaron." she said as he followed behind her.

i shook my head as i got up and grabbed the pain medicine she gave me popping two pills in my mouth and swallowed them dry.

i walked to my room and turned on my playstation before grabbing my phone.

xylah: azaire

-yeah

xylah: wyd

-finna get on the game, wassup?

xylah: nun i'm just bored rn

-what you been doing today?

while i waiting on her to respond i went to my night stand and pulled out a small bag of weed and the gars i had before my phone started ringing.

"yoooo.." i answered putting it on speaker.

"gang! fuck you doing??" i heard benz voice.

"i'm tryna roll up r-right now, wassup?" i said as i placed the weed in the grinder.

"you should come thru later to this block party near the apartments." he said.

"i'll see, i'm a lil handicapped right now." i said and he laughed.

"that lil ass bullet wound bring yo ass dawg, and bring yo shawty so she can know the girls more." he said and i shook my head.

"ion k-know if she gonna wanna come but i'll probably come." i said before hanging up.

xylah: reading and crocheting, i made coco a lil skirt

-be playing dress up wit that damn pig

xylah: hush she likes it

i laughed some before i started rolling up, my bedroom door opened showing my dad,"aye i'm finna take yo mama out...don't be letting hooligans in my house." he said and i shook my head.

"imma probably go out later..." i told him and he nodded.

"ight be careful tho...just got in that shootout earlier." he said in a lower voice.

"i will." i said before he walked back out.

my phone started ringing and i saw xylah calling me on facetime, i answered and her eye was in the camera.

"you always answer in the m-most weird ways." i said and she pulled the camera back showing her face.

"yo hair??" i asked seeing it was in an afro.

"hush im waiting for my ma to come back with my wig." she said pushing her glasses up on her face.

i hummed in response before lighting my blunt,"you always smoking." she said and i shrugged.

"oh later on i'm going to this block party i-if you wanna come wit me." i said and i saw her smile a lil before taking her face out the camera.

"i will but- you have to bring me starbucks and come over." she said and i raised my eyebrows.

"ight i gotchu, i'll be over there in a f-few hours." i said and she nodded.

i stepped out the car holding xylah's drink and a bouquet of orange tulips for her.

i looked around before taking my gun out my waistband and placed it underneath my seat.

i walked up to the door and knocked on it, the door opened revealing her lil brothers.

"why the hell yall opening doors?" i heard namari say walking to the door.

"oh- take y'all bad asses to the living room." she told them and they laughed running off.

"follow me." she said and i followed behind her until we stopped at a bedroom and she knocked on the door.

xylah's head peaked out and i noticed she had on a burgundy wig with a band around her head.

"hey azaire!" she said and gave me a quick hug surprising me a lil.

"damn i'm here too." namari said and xylah eyed her.

"i already spoke to you today." she said before pulling me in her room.

"awee thank you, you really got my drink." she said grabbing her drink then the flowers.

"they're prettyyyy, thank you." she said looking up at me and i noticed her cheeks were a lil red.

"you're welcome ma..." i said and watched her place the flowers on her dresser along with her drink.

"what happened to your arm??" she asked pointing at my bandage.

"i just hurt myself h-helping my dad out earlier." i said and she nodded her head.

i sat down on the edge of her bed while she sat at her vanity and took off the band on her hair, i watched as she combed the straight hair and made it a straight middle part.

"how long is that??" i asked noticing it was definitely pass her ass.

"ion know...i just chose the longest option." she said and i watched her fix edges on it.

once it was how she liked she wrapped the band back around her head,"okay what should i wear??" she asked and i shrugged.

"that's up to you." i said as she got up and went to her closet.

"mmm...hold this!" she said and threw a shirt at me.

i shook my head holding it up, it was grey with long sleeves, cropped, and had to be tied in the front.

all her stomach and titties finna be out....

she grabbed a pair of jean shorts...that were short. then a pair of grey dunks. "you think this good?" she asked and i nodded.

she grabbed the shirt from me then went to her bathroom to change.

i had on black sweatpants and a black compression shirt with black air forces, i ran my hands over my waves as i waited for her to come out.

the bathroom door opened and she came out in the outfit she chose and she looked good as fuck.

"you look pretty ma..." i told her and she smiled.

"thank you....i wanted to tell you, you looked good when you first came in but i ain't know what all was gonna come out namari mouth." she said making me laugh.

i watched her grab her phone then she opened a bag pulling out makeup, i went on my phone to entertain myself until she was ready.

about 15 minutes later she called my name making me look up and see she was staring at me,"you ready??" i asked and she nodded making me get up.

i watched as she put a charm bracelet on her wrist then a necklace around her neck that had her initial on it.

i let her walk out and i followed behind her as she walked to the kitchen where her parents were,"mama we finna go." she said and they both looked over at us.

"aweee you look beautiful baby, you look good as well azaire." her mama said me.

"what you mean he look good??" namari asked eyeing her.

"namari please don't start."

xylah laughed quietly before grabbing my hand and pulled me out the kitchen.

# Chapter 8

♥

**X**ylah sailor summer

i placed my earbuds in my ear as azaire parked the car, i could hear the loud music and people as we were pulling up.

"xylah- listen." he said turning towards me and i paid attention to him taking in his appearance.

the way his shirt was hugging his body and showing off his abs and muscles, he had gotten a haircut recently, he had on a few chains around his neck and stud earrings in his ear.

"yo?" he said snapping me out my daze.

"i'm sorry..." i mumbled looking away.

"i was saying...stay close and if at anytime...you f-feel uncomfortable let me know and we can leave. don't smoke nun if you didn't see t-them roll it, or drink anything somebody give you unless you watch them the whole t-time. my friends here too also." he said and i nodded before getting out the car.

i walked to his side and noticed him messing with his waistband and shirt, he looked at me and raised his eyebrow.

"i can open my own door." i said knowing what he was already thinking.

"this one time." he said as he started walking and i stayed by him.

"YOOO!" taylin yelled gaining azaire's attention.

we walked over to them and they all dapped each other up,"hey girl." ayani said and i looked over at her and sage giving them a smile small.

"hey." i said quietly.

"girl you don't have to be shy wit us." sage said.

"literally they just some hoodrats." taylin shrugged and sage mushed his head.

"don't start." she said flipping her braids over her shoulder.

"nigga- you on that timing tonight??" benz asked holding up a bottle of casamigos.

"shittt...." azaire said grabbing the bottle.

i watched as he opened it and waterfall a good bit in his mouth before handing it back, he swallowed it all and shook his head.

"y'all asses better not be getting sloppy drunk out here." ayani said shaking her head.

"girl you done had 5 shots of henny and now you smoking..." benz said and she shrugged.

"i know my limit." she said waving him off.

"ion know about y'all but i'm hungry." sage said getting up from taylin's lap.

"it's them munchies." benz pointed out and she waved him off.

"y'all wanna come wit me?" she asked me and ayani.

ayani nodded her head and i looked up at azaire who was already looking at me,"you can go if you want pretty." he said and i smiled feeling my face beat up.

"and don't y'all corrupt our new friend wit y'all ways." benz said and they waved him off.

"hush." ayani said and i walked with them to another part of the place where i saw grills and older people cooking.

"sooo xylah." sage started and i looked at her as they grabbed plates and handed me one.

"you and azaire?" she said.

"what?" i asked and they laughed.

"so y'all together or what?" ayani asked and i shrugged.

"i don't know..." i mumbled.

"well i can see he likes you, that's all imma say about it." ayani said and sage nodded.

"y'all would be cute, plus your so fuckin gorgeous girl." sage said and i smiled a lil.

"thanks." i said and she nodded.

we got food to eat then sat at some wood benches to chill and eat,"what kinda sodas y'all want?" sage asked getting up.

"sprite." i said and ayani agreed.

"make it two." ayani said before sage walked towards the cooler.

it was going on 11pm and now we were chilling at taylin's car. they were all under some kind of influence including weed and alcohol.

the only thing i did was smoke half a blunt that azaire rolled, but that was it.

but the drunkest were probably benz and sage.

i was starting to get more comfortable around them and honestly i was glad.

azaire had the door opened and was laying down in the backseat with his legs out the car, i was sitting on one of them i had got tired of standing.

sage and ayani were sitting on the trunk of the car while benz and taylin were shooting dice wit some other boys nearby.

i looked back at azaire and saw he was asleep making me laugh some,"azaire..." i called and gently tapped his chest.

he didn't budge,"azaire." i said a lil louder and he groaned.

"hollon i gotchu sis, get up real quick tho." benz said and i was hesitant but i got up.

"aye nigga some dude tryna get xylah number." he said into the car and i watched azaire quickly sit up and his hand go to his waistband.

"man...y'all niggas play too much." he grumbled seeing i was right in front of him.

"man wake yo ass up! cant hang fa shit." benz laughed.

azaire got up out the car and shook his head, i looked back at his waistband and noticed a black handle of-

i tapped azaire and he looked down at me, i pointed at it,"what about it?" he asked and i just looked at him confused before shaking my head.

i watched as he fixed it to be less noticeable, "last drop??" taylin asked holding the casamigos towards azaire.

"man keep that..." he said making them laugh.

"thank you." ayani said grabbing it and drunk the last bit.

"you ight?" azaire asked me quietly and i nodded as i looked up at him.

his eyes were low and slightly red,"are you?" i asked him and he licked his lips before answering.

"yeah." he said before looking away from me.

i watched his eyes squint before he looked over at taylin and benz,"aye...y'all see that shit too." he said and they both looked the direction he was just looking in.

"man i ain't wit this bullshit tonight...i'm drunk as shit too." benz said as he leaned off the car and lifted his shirt up taking out a gun and cocked it back making my eyes widen.

"bruh chill." taylin quickly said and i watched as sage and ayani got down from the trunk.

"gone head in the house." taylin told sage who nodded.

their apartment was walking distance so, "xylah go wit them." azaire said as he pulled his gun out as well his eyes focused on whoever he was looking at.

i wanted to say something but i decided against it before following sage and ayani,"you good??" ayani asked as i walked between them.

as we walked the music was fading out in the background, i only nodded my head continuing to look down.

so his job wit his dad....?

"lemme guess you ain't know." sage said and i nodded again.

it fell into awkward silence, i guess they didn't know what else to say and i didn't either.

we made it to her apartment and sage allowed us in first before closing and locking the door.

"whew shit...bitch the world spinning..." sage said once she sat down and ayani laughed.

"i'll get us some water." ayani said before walking to the kitchen.

sage laid on the couch she was on while i sat on the chair that reclined, i occupied myself on my phone before i grabbed the water bottle ayani handed me.

i opened it and took a few sips since i did have cotton mouth from smoking, they had turned something on on tv but i was stuck in my phone.

-are you ok???-azairedelivered.

i chewed on my lip and ignored the feeling in my stomach as i went to tiktok to distract my self.

the door opened and the boys piled in,"y'all coo??" sage asked as they came in silently.

"get up." azaire told me and i eyed him before standing up, he sat down where i was then pulled me down in his lap.

my back was against the arm of the chair as my legs went across his lap,"them niggas wasn't doing shit but talking..." benz said as he sat down.

"they be tryna act big and bad but scared as soon as you pull a gun out...they asses acting for other muthafuckas knowing they ain't built for this damn life." taylin said as he put sage's feet in his lap to sit down.

i looked at azaire and he was staring at nothing in particular as one of his hands was rubbing my thighs, i got a tingly feeling between my legs but i ignored it.

"you good?" i asked him quietly and his eyes snapped to mines.

"yeah...m-my bad..." he said shaking his head looking away.

i gently grabbed his chin and turned his face towards me,"you could've told me..." i said quiet enough for him to hear.

"i didn't want to scare y-you away.." he said looking down in his lap.

i sighed and laid my head on his shoulder,"i feel safe with you." i admitted.

# Chapter 9

♥

**X**ylah sailor summer

it's been a few days since the party, and i was starting to actually text the girls more and talk on the phone with them sometimes.

i grabbed my tote bag and put a change of clothes inside along with some bathroom necessities. i currently had on white sweatpants and a white tank top that was cropped.

i slipped on my slides then used a claw clip to pin up my hair, i made sure i had everything i needed just for a night then grabbed my phone.

i let my mom know i was leaving since she was the only one home,"y'all been hanging out a lot..." she said looking me up and down.

"ma..." i said and she laughed waving me off.

i went to my car and started it after texting azaire.

-do you want sumn from starbucks

azaire: get me whatever you get, when you get here the door should be unlocked

-i'm not just gonna walk in

azaire: lmk when you outside

i put my phone up and pulled out the driveway before making my way towards starbucks.

"mama..." azaire said leading me into the kitchen where his mom was at.

"mama this xylah, xylah this my mama." he said introducing us and his mama smiled at me.

"girl you're even prettier in person, how'd you end up wit my son??" she asked and azaire smacked his lips.

"thanks and umm just at the library at the same time..." i said and she nodded.

"okay well it's nice meeting you, i'm cooking now so it should be done soon. y'all have fun." she said.

azaire lead me to his bedroom and closed the door behind him,"where's your dad?" i asked.

"he's out right now...he'll be b-back when the food done." he said sitting in his game chair while i sat on the bed.

"so...are you staying the night??" he asked and i nodded.

"umm...can you read wit me? before you really get into the game." i asked and he turned his chair towards the bed and placed his controller down.

"what book i-is it??" he asked as i crossed my legs and took the book out my bag.

"it's actually a book with poetry, it's called milk and honey." i told him and he got up to sit beside me.

his room was already naturally dark due to the blackout curtains over his windows, only light coming from the tv.

"you can read it, i'll listen." he said and i nodded as i picked up from where i was.

i read about 15 pages then looked at him making sure he was still awake, he looked back at me and smiled making me smile.

"yo ass blushing." he said and i looked away from him closing the book.

"whatever.." i mumbled and he laughed before scooping me up in his arms making me cling to him.

"what you doing?" i asked as he sat in his gaming chair keeping me in his lap.

i relaxed against him as he grabbed his controller then handed me one,"what-"

"we g-gonna play mortal kombat." he cut me off, we clicked the game then we both picked our own characters.

"ready to lose??" he asked and i rolled my eyes.

"yeahhh think that." i said as the battle started.

"yeahhh my girl tearing yo ass up." i said and just then he did his special move on my character killing her immediately.

i sat the controller down and got out his lap while he laughed,"xylah." he said as i laid on his bed and grabbed my bag pulling out my headphones.

"move imma watch spongebob..." i mumbled as he laid beside me.

"you mad you l-lost?" he asked and i shook my head no.

"you lying." he said and i nodded before pressing play on my phone.

i felt him move around to see him laying on his back and staring at me, i paused my show,"what?" i asked.

he pulled me on top of him and wrapped his arms around me,"azaire you like me right?" i asked him and his eyebrows furrowed before he nodded his head.

"w-why you ask?"

"cause....i don't know nevermind..." i mumbled.

"nah tell me what's on your mind." he said and i sighed.

"ion knoww like...we haven't really done much or a lot of intimate stuff..." i said picking at my nails.

"cause....right now we j-just chilling and getting to know each other, i wanna m-make you mines officially before we start doing allat..." he said and i nodded.

"is that okay with you?" he asked.

"yeah...i'm sorry." i said and he shook his head grabbing my chin.

"it's fine, whenever you overthinking s-shit just tell me ight?" i nodded my head as he sat up and now i was straddling his lap.

"azaire! xylah! the food ready!" his mama yelled making me get up off him and i noticed the bulge in his sweats.

"eyes up here." he said making me look up at him.

i groaned as i found myself waking up then looked over at azaire, he looked like he was sweating and his eyes were shut tightly. his whole body seemed tensed as he turned on his side.

he was mumbling incoherent words, i sat up and gently shook him,"azaire...azaire..." i said and he turned the opposite way of me pushing my hands back.

"n-no- i c-can't...." he mumbled wrapping his arms around himself.

"azaire get up!" i raised my voice a lil and he jumped up breathing hard as he looked around the room before his eyes landed on me.

"shit...m-my b-bad..." he said as he pressed his hands against his eyes then pushed the cover off of him.

i watched as he got up and walked to the bathroom closing the door behind him, i sat in the bed for a few seconds before forcing myself to get up i had on one of his t-shirts and it came pass mid-thigh.

i softly knocked on the door, he opened it then leaned back against the sink as i closed the door and looked up at him.

he still was sweating a lil and his face was flushed, his eyes looked glossy.

"are you okay?" i asked quietly and he nodded.

"no you're not..." i said and he shook his head.

"it had a n-nightmare, i ain't m-mean to wake you up." he said and i moved around him to turn on the cold water.

"splash some water on your face..." i told him and he listened bending down closer to the sink.

i pointed at his towel once he was done and he used it to dry his face off.

"you wanna talk about it?" i asked.

it was sumn namari and my mom would always ask me whenever i would get upset or overwhelmed.

"ion know- imma j-just stutter a lot...it's gonna s-sound like gibberish." he explained.

"just talk in shorter sentences, take breaks while explaining whenever you get overwhelmed and try to relax." i said and he turned his head to the side slightly.

"you be listening..." he said.

"when i t-tell you the stuff my therapist b-be saying...you actually listened." he said and i nodded unsure what to say.

"am i not supposed to?" i asked and he quickly shook his head.

"no just....no one has ever d-done that before." he said and i grabbed his hand leading him back to his bed.

he got back comfortable in his bed while i did the same, i stared at the ceiling until he started talking.

"umm...when i w-was 7 we lived in a different house, and at the time i didn't exactly know about the shit my dad was doing....one n-night i could hear my mama screaming and it woke me up

when i walked out my room it was t-this man with a mask and he held a gun to my head and i j-just froze...i couldn't scream or a-anything but my mama was still screaming

that's when the dude forced me into my parents room...my dad wasn't at h-home at the time and...i c-couldn't help her, they just took t-turns beating her in front of me, one of them g-gave me a gun and t-told me to shoot her

when i refused they hit me across the head and i c-could feel the blood leaking down my face...then gunshots rang out and my d-dad finally appeared...he threw his gun to the ground and picked me up...my mama was unconscious i just remember how she looked...

it's engraved in m-my head and i hate that i couldn't do shit...i only stood there x-xylah..." he finished and my heart ached for him.

"azaire...you were only 7, it was a 7 year old vs grown ass men...with guns that was never a fair fight to begin with." i told him and i reached over to wipe his tears.

"that's w-why i'm in the whole speech therapy shit....after that night i didn't talk for a y-year straight..and for the longest it was b-broken sentences." he explained and i gently rubbed his face.

"then when i turned about 13...my dad really introduced me to what he did and the other dangers that came with it...when m-my mama found out she was pissed....literally last week she was because she had to stitch my w-wound...

my dad did his best to try and lie but my mama isn't dumb....she b-believes that i just pitch in here and there, but honestly it's an almost everyday thing. that's why i ain't wanna tell you about it at first..nothing good comes from this street shit...

so i could get if you didn't wanna really still t-talk to me, in this shit all you really get is jail or death.." he said and i pursed my lips together.

"azaire....i really like you and i'm gonna take whatever comes with you just....when you do certain stuff can you try and be smart about it? do you think this is sumn you would want to do for the rest of your life??" i asked and he shook his head no.

"nah...by time i'm in my 20s i'd probably get all the money i've received from this shit cleaned first then buy my own house and invest in a business and find legal work." he said and i nodded.

"well...it sounds like you have a plan you jus gotta work towards it." i said before yawning and he laughed quietly.

"go to sleep ma." he said and i instantly placed my head against the pillow before i felt him pull me on top of him.

i laid my head on his chest and got comfortable, his arms wrapped around my back and i felt him kiss the top of my head before fixing my bonnet.

"thank you.." he said but i was already half asleep so i didn't respond.

# Chapter 10

♥

**X**ylah sailor summer

i placed a bookmark in my book as my bedroom door opened and i was met with the twins but kamari had tears on his face.

"xylah- that boy down the street pushed kamari." jamari said and his face was slightly red.

i could tell he was pissed,"kamari come here." i said sitting up and he walked over to me.

i helped him on my bed and jamari,"your knee a lil scraped up but you should be okay— what you do? cause i know yo evil ass." i said to jamari and he did that lil smirk namari be doing.

"umm i kicked his dick...then threw that big rock at his head and stomped his stomach." he said and i just stared at him for a few seconds before scooting over a lil.

"unt unt...yo ass might be a serial killer or sumn.." i mumbled as i grabbed a bandaid for kamari's knee.

i put hydrogen peroxide on it first then the bandaid,"have mama look at it too." i told him and they carefully slid off my bed.

"can we take coco??" kamari asked pointing at her in the corner who was laying on her back asleep.

"i mean if you can carry her sure." i said and i watched as he struggled and she started snorting loudly.

"stop torturing that damn pig." namari said stopping at my room door.

"i'm not hush." kamari said and walked out with her.

"xylah- you thought about what you wanna do for your birthday?" she asked and i shrugged.

"i gotta idea then....that morning you go out to eat wit us and immediate family, you can invite your lil boyfriend if you want-"

"he's not my boyfriend." i cut her off and she looked me up and down.

"like i was saying invite your boyfriend- then you can spend the rest of the day doing whatever you want except you have to get out the house.." she finished.

"okay...that's fine with me." i said shrugging.

"mhm...send me some stuff you gonna want- also tell yo boyfriend come over...i needa get some more weed off him..." she said and i rolled my eyes.

"i feel that's the only reason you like him." i said.

"no.....i can see he makes you happy and he's brought you out your shell some, you actually go out now and not just the library. the weed just a good plus." she said then walked my room closing the door.

azaire: yk namari text me bout some weed??

-why y'all got each other number?

azaire: not every question needs an answer

-bitch

azaire liked 'bitch'

-really???read-azaire???read-can you at least lmk if you coming over or notdelivered

"bitch ass..." i mumbled as i grabbed my rat tail comb to scratch underneath my wig.

i went to my closet and grabbed an oversized grey tshirt that had the powerpuff girls on it and matched it with pink shorts that were high waisted and came mid-thigh.

i was in my mama room watching a movie with her as we ate snacks, the door opened revealing namari and azaire.

both looking high as hell....

"your such a bad influence." mama said shaking her head.

"whattt?? accusations." namari said as she walked in the room then laid on my mama making me mug her.

"girl- get off her." i said and namari flipped me off.

"go to yo room, i wanna be wit my wife." she said and i shook my head getting up and closed their door.

i grabbed azaire's hand and pulled him to my bedroom,"azaire!" i heard kamari yell then him and jamari ran to azaire.

"wassup lil niggas." azaire said smiling and squatted down to their level.

"did you order the hot wheels set?" jamari asked and he nodded.

"yeah and i got y'all some m-more cars too, they gonna be here by the end of this week. i'll let y'all sister know when t-they get here." he told them and they nodded.

"okay! thank you." jamari said and they both went back to their rooms.

"now why you buying them allat?? they don't need no more of them cars." i said walking in my room and plopped on my bed.

"cause i remember being they age, and i would be happy as hell w-when a muthafucka bought me shit i wanted." he said and i shook my head.

he stood at the end of my bed and i watched as he pulled off his hoodie, his shirt slightly lifting showing his v-line and his psd boxers band.

he had on ripped jeans and a white tshirt, i noticed the plastic wrap around his lower arm.

"what's that?" i asked pointing at it then he sat on my bed beside me.

"i gotta tattoo after my therapy session..." he said and i grabbed his upper arm to get a better look at it.

it was tiger eyes with a clock and roses,"it looks cool." i said as i slightly turned his arm.

"you can t-take it off." he said and told me how to take it off and i did so carefully.

"i think i want one..." i said and looked at him seeing him already staring at me.

"well yo birthday coming up...you can get it then, i'll hook y-you up with my artist." he said and i nodded.

"i'll have to ask my parents to make sure but i might want it like a few days before my birthday." i said and he grabbed my ipad and unlocked it before going to bet+.

"you look good." i said as he laid back against my headboard.

"preciate it ma, yo bare face beautiful as shit." he said licking over his lips and my face heated up as he stared at me then back at the ipad screen.

i had been chilling at home today so i didn't have any makeup or lashes on.

"you k-know what you doing for yo birthday yet?" he asked as he placed my ipad down and i noticed he had a movie ready to play.

"welll in the morning time imma be wit my family and go out to eat...ion know what imma do the rest of the day tho but i know i should get out the house." i said and noticed he seemed zoned out before speaking.

"what if i p-plan sumn for you?" he asked.

"you'd do that??" i asked and he nodded.

"y-yeah...i'd run the plans by your parents first, and if you want i can invite benz and em." he suggested and i smiled while nodding.

"ight, i'm not gonna tell you what imma do tho...you'll f-find out that afternoon." he said and i groaned.

"whyyy?" i whined falling back against the bed on my back.

"cause i wanna surprise you, chill out." he said pulling me closer beside him.

i stared at his face and noticed his eyes were low and slightly red as he stared back at me,"bruh why you l-looking at me like that?" he asked raising one of his eyebrows.

"cause you look sexy." i said and he chuckled.

"gone bruh..." he said pressing play and i started watching whatever movie he had put on for us.

# Chapter 11

♥

**X**ylah sailor summer

it's a week before my birthday and i was more excited then usual, probably because i was actually doing more for my birthday besides being with my family.

and i love them but now i actually have some friends to hang out with...and my man that's not my man.

my phone went off and i checked the group chat with jus the girls.

sage: y'all better be readyyyy

ayani:bitch i'm just waking up

-i just got out the shower

sage: y'all got 30 minutes before i pull up to get y'all we going to the mall

ayani: who said i had shopping money

sage: girl

ayani: OKAY IM GETTING IN THE SHOWER NEOW

-lemme know when you otw

i put my phone down and dried off before putting on lotion, i put on grey flare leggings that were low waisted and a black shirt that was cropped with black crocs.

azaire: wyd ma
-just finished getting ready
azaire: you going wit sage and ayani??
-yeah
azaire:check yo cash app
i went out messages and checked my notifications
cashapp azaire sent you $300.

i decided to call him and he answered with a blunt between his lips,"why you send that much?" i asked and he shrugged.

"y'all going s-shopping right?" he asked and i nodded my head.

"ight then use it..." he said and i eyed the camera.

"but i have my own-"

"xylah i ain't ask allat, use the money." he said and i raised my eyebrow.

"fine....wanna see my outfit??" i asked him and he nodded.

i put my phone up on my bathroom counter then stepped back ,"mm...you look good, lemme get a 360." he said and i also noticed he hasn't been stuttering as much lately.

i did a quick spin before grabbing my gel and hairbrush, my natural hair was out i was letting it breathe since next week i was getting a new wig.

"should i do a high puff or low puff?" i asked him as i watched him blow out smoke.

"low, but do t-two of em." he said and i nodded.

i parted my hair down the middle and hoped my part was straight enough, how it looked in the back got nun to do wit me.

i used enough gel on both sides of my head then brushed down my hair, once it was slick enough i grabbed the hair ties putting them in.

i did simple edges cause my arms were already tired from trying to get it slick, i did light makeup and put on lashes.

i put lipgloss on my lips and saw azaire taking facetime photos, i shook my head grabbing my phone.

i made sure i had my earbuds in my pocket.

"you still wanna go get yo tattoos today??" he asked as i sat down on my bed and put my card in my phone case.

"yeah, can we get starbucks before?" i asked and he laughed lightly.

"yo ass addicted t-to starbucks." he said and i shrugged.

"ma pleaseeee." i begged my mama on the phone.

me and the girls had just left the mall, i bought myself some clothes, a small bit of lingerie from victoria's secret, and two pairs of shoes.

now we ended up at a piercings shop,"xylah you can get your belly pierced but the tongue piercing pushing it...." she said.

"what if i still get it...?" i asked.

"imma beat yo ass, xylah you don't need that."

"i know i don't need it but i really want it." i whined and she rolled her eyes.

"you know that's gonna be a healing process right?? like you gonna struggle to eat certain foods and what not..."she said and i sighed.

"fine..." i mumbled about to hang up.

"get the piercing and fix yo face." she said before hanging up.

"girl you spoiled." sage laughed and i shrugged as i got called back.

"wait one of y'all come wit me." i quickly said and they both came.

"so you want the top of your belly pierced, and snake bites?"

i nodded my head at the lady as she grabbed the different jewelry and tools,"chose which one you would like." she said handing me a small box with belly rings.

after 15 minutes i was done and paid to leave,"how much the tongue hurt?" sage asked.

"not gonna lie it was a lil painful but the belly wasn't too bad." i said.

sage got both sides of her nose pierced and ayani got her septum....we all got our bellies pierced.

"okay y'all wanna get food then go home?" ayani asked.

"yeah but can you actually drop me off at azaire's??" i asked and sage nodded.

"yess i'll take you to your man pooh." she said and i shook my head.

"xylah...." azaire called as i walked infront of him making me turn around.

"hmm??"

"come here and o-open yo mouth." he said and i did so.

"you like it?" i asked and he nodded licking his lips.

"definitely....you didn't t-tell me you was getting yo tongue pierced." he said and we walked into a shop that played low jazz music.

i shrugged as i looked around.

"wassup azaire, you here on time." a dude at the front desk said.

"of course, syd ready?" he asked grabbing my hand and pulling me closer to him.

"yeah head on back." azaire lead me down a hall to a door that was already open.

"wassup syd." azaire said and the girl turned around with a smirk on his face.

"wassup nigga- this shawty?" she said looking at me...but with more of lust.

"yes- stop looking at her like that." azaire said slightly shoving her and syd laughed.

"my bad- aye he don't do you right you can always come to me." she said and i pursed my lips.

"syd-" azaire started.

"i'm fuckin wit youuu! have a seat sexy and i'll get the stencils i made." she said before walking out the room.

i sat on the chair that was leaned back and waited for her to come back while azaire got on his phone.

"azaire." i said catching his attention and he looked over at me.

"can you stay the night wit me??" i asked him and he nodded.

"yeah i'll make s-sure my parents cool wit it." he said making me smile.

"how many tattoos you getting??" he asked me and i pursed my lips together.

"you asking as if i didn't send you the ones i wanted..." i said and he shrugged.

"alright you used any numbing cream or anything?" syd asked coming back in the room with gloves on and stencils in her hand.

i shook my head no,"wow...first tattoos and you just going all out huh?" she asked and i nodded my head yes.

once she had her stencils in place and cleaned the area she started doing the tattoo, and honestly it didn't hurt as bad as i thought i would. it's just a prick repeatedly going into your skin, yeah some parts had more pressure but it wasn't anything to crazy.

"you definitely went o-overboard with the tattoos..." azaire said as we pulled up to my house.

we had just left his house where he grabbed some stuff to stay the night,"i don't think so, i just got a lot at once. " i said.

on the side of my left boob i got a small sized heart, i got the word sonder on my right wrist, made in heaven was on my lower back in the middle it wasn't anything huge, and finally think positive on my left wrist with a cross as the t.

"i'm still mad you wouldn't let me get the other tattoo..." i said as we walked to the front door.

"xylah...you w-wanted bite me on yo ass cheek..." he grumbled as i unlocked the door.

"okay? you was gonna be the only one to see it..." i mumbled lowly.

he didn't respond back as i lead him to my room but of course he was stopped by the twins, i swear they be more happy to see him then me.

i walked to my parents room knocking before walking in.

"i'm scared....i hope you ain't take after me." namari said with her eyes closed and my mama shook her head.

"come on lemme see em." my mama said pausing her tv show.

i walked to her side and she looked at my arms.

"okay okay cute...where's the rest i know you." she said and i laughed lifting up my shirt just a lil bit so she could see the heart.

"mmm...that's not too bad only gonna be seen when you wearing sumn very short or revealing." she said and that caught namari attention.

"why is you letting an tattoo artist tat yo titty?" she asked.

"namari all them tattoos you got while in jail- hush." my mama said and i turned around to show them the last-

"see i'm finna grab sand paper.." i heard namari mumble.

"it's not even nun crazy- girl shut up. it's cute baby and make sure you clean your piercings and what not, and take care of them tattoos." my mama said shooing me out the room.

"wait- where azaire? my weed..." namari said and i shook my head.

"her boyfriend is not yo weed person..." mama said and namari waved her off.

"girl that's that delusion you speaking." namari said then azaire walked in and handed her a bag of weed.

"i already sent you the money on cashapp- you wanna smoke wit me?" namari asked making azaire laugh.

"you just smoked an hour ago..." mama said glaring at namari.

"and you was smoking this morning..." i told azaire.

i watched as him and namari both shrugged.

"mom!mom!" both the twins ran in the room jamari stopping at namari and pointed at the bag of weed.

"get you some business, what y'all want?" namari asked putting the weed on the nightstand.

"can we watch a movie?" kamari asked.

"in who room?" namari asked and the twins gave her a really look.

"guess y'all will have a smoke sesh later." i told azaire and slipped out the room with him behind me.

we went to my room and shut the door as i grabbed clothes,"it's cool i use yo shower?" azaire asked and i nodded my head.

he went to the bathroom and i just changed into a pair of hello kitty pajama pants and a pink tube top before getting into my bed, i took out my earbuds and waited for him.

i saw coco in her bed she was asleep so i got back up and went to pet her gently so she wouldn't wake up, i replaced her old water with fresh water and a few cut up carrots in her bowl of food.

she'll wake up in the middle of the night and eat.

finally azaire came back out the bathroom, he only had on plaid pajama pants that were black and white.

my eyes instantly went to his v-line and abs, i could feel my mouth watering at the sight-

what's going on with me?

my eyes looked over the tattoos on his body as he put on his black durag,"oh i got y-you an early birthday present." he said going into his bag.

he handed me a small package that was flat in a way, i sat on my bed and waited for him to do the same before i opened it.

a smile instantly found its way on my face as i looked at the bonnet, it was customized with my name on it and had a few pictures of us on it.

"aweeee it's so cute, thank youuu!" i said hugging him and he pulled me on top of him hugging me back.

i smiled and kissed his cheek and i could see his face turn red a little.

"you're welcome ma..." he replied with a smile on his face.

sumn in me wanna ride yo face...

i quickly shook my head feeling a throb between my legs,"we r-reading anything tonight?" he asked and i quickly nodded getting up.

i took my hair out the puffs it was in then put on the bonnet he gave me,"hollon stand right there a-and smile." he said and i did as told before a flash went off.

i playfully rolled my eyes and grabbed a book from my bookshelf before laying in bed and he laid beside me,"okay this is to kill a mockingbird." i said and watched his eyebrow furrow.

"i think i read t-that shit in middle school." he said and i nodded.

"me too...i just wanna read it again now that i'm a lil older." i said getting comfortable under my cover.

"you wanna take turn reading pages?" i asked.

"i can try..." he said and i smiled.

"thanks." i said and kissed his cheek again.

when i pulled back he grabbed my chin this time kissing my lips only for a quick second.

my face instantly heats up and i get that familiar feeling inbetween my legs again.

"why you looking like that?" he asked me and i shook my head opening the book.

"xylah..." he said covering the back with his hand.

"umm...it was my first kiss..." i said lowly but loud enough for him to hear.

"mmm....yo lips soft as shit." he said and i lightly laughed.

"can i get another?" i asked and he nodded leaning back towards me.

i instantly closed the space between us pressing my lips against his, i almost forgot about the book until he pulled it from me and pulled me on top of him.

our lips moved against each other in sync and i felt his tongue swipe against my bottom lip, i pulled back and he stared at me with low eyes.

"what?" i asked and he chuckled shaking his head.

"nun ma, we reading or no?" he said placing the book in my hand and i sat up straddling him since he was still laying down.

i nodded my head and felt sumn poking me making me get off him and lay back beside him.

the way i was prepared to sin.

# Chapter 12

♥

**A**zaire kade carmine

 i passed the blunt over to benz,"you can have the rest of that." i told him as i got on my phone.

 "damn you foreal? like it's still half left." he asked and i nodded.

 "it's good, i'm not tryna g-get too high finna hang out wit my girl..." i said then i heard a cough.

 i looked at taylin and waited for him to speak,"you said my girl— you wasn't feeling xylah??" he asked and i rolled my eyes.

 "nigga i'm t-talking about her." i said and his mouth dropped into a 'o' shape.

 "oh hell, i'm high as fuck." he said shaking his head.

 "was finna say...you know his ass ain't coming up off her, his ass been on her real bad. ain't never seen you hang out wit a girl so damn much." benz said and i paid them no attention.

 they wasn't lying but still, i felt sumn different with xylah...sumn real i couldn't explain, she was the only person i've opened up to about my stuttering.

everybody else i told it was just sumn that started happening, xylah made me feel safe and secure...i couldn't explain it. she made me feel good about myself.

xylah: azaireee ion know how to dress

-just put on some clothes ma

xylah: like whatttt?? fancy? chill? bummy? comfy?

-casual?

xylah: what a ? like...how do you not know when you've planned the date

-ight put on sumn casual and comfortable

xylah: okayy thank you, wyd?

-rn i'm wit benz and taylin, wyd

xylah: finna get in the shower and start getting ready, how should i do my hair??

-that's up to you pretty, whatever you feel like doing

xylah: imma send you options when i get out the shower and you choose one

-okayread

i put my phone back up before chilling wit the boys for a few more minutes before getting up,"imma see y'all around-"

"you'll see us this weekend actually for shawty lil birthday shit." taylin said.

"ain't nun LIL about everything he got planned for her." benz said as he finished off the blunt.

"i didn't even do a lot.." i mumbled and benz scoffed.

"boyyyy- how much money you spent on just the first day?" he asked and i shrugged.

"don't matter, i just know she gonna enjoy it." i said making sure i had my keys and lighter before leaving.

i was pulling into xylah's driveway and she was already walking out the door, i bet you she was stalking my location.

my eyes looked over her appearance and almost immediately i felt blood rush to my crotch. she had on tight black cargo pants with a cropped white long sleeve sweater and white air forces.

her hair was blown out and in a messy bun on top of her head, she wasn't wearing any makeup or lashes just lipgloss.

yeah my girl raw.

she opened the car door and immediately smiled staring at the bouquet in the passenger seat along with her favorite drink from starbucks in the cup holder on her side.

"awe- azaire." she said pouting and i laughed a lil at her face.

she got in the car and held the pink roses in her lap while smiling as she shut the door, she leaned over the console and placed a peck on my lips.

"thank you, a lot." she said and i nodded pulling out her driveway.

"it's no problem....you l-look pretty as fuck." i told her and i saw her cheeks turn a light red.

"yet again- thank you." she said and we shared a laugh.

she took a sip of her drink and i instantly saw a smile across her face as she drunk more.

we stopped at a red light and i watched her take a picture of herself and the flowers i got her before posting it.

"azaire..." she started and i hummed.

"does it ever bother you like.....i haven't really bought you anything and you always spoiling me..." she said.

"i spoil you cause i w-want to, i'm not expecting nun back....i like you for you not what you can g-give me. plus i don't care about you buying me shit, i like that you there for me and how we vibe with each other." i told her and she nodded and started picking at her nails.

"you sure?" she asked and i smiled over at her.

"i promise ma, you good." i said and pecked her lips before the light turned green and i focused back on the road.

"if i buy you sumn are you gonna accept it?" she asked and i nodded.

"of course, i'm just saying don't f-feel like you have to." i said putting my hand on her thigh.

"okay...where we going?" she asked.

"you'll see when we get there..." i said and she tilted her head to the side.

"ight ight...top golf, then we getting sumn to eat....and the last p-place we staying there till the morning." i told her.

"and i'm letting you choose w-where we eat at, i know yo picky ass." i said and she laughed.

"lord...i'm full as fuck...why you let me eat all this?" she asked as she rubbed her stomach.

we went to top golf and it was fun until xylah accidentally let her club go too and it hit a person that worked there. so we just quickly left.

we just left the restaurant she picked out which sold soul food so we both were full honestly, even took some peach cobbler to go.

"you wanted to ma, who am i t-to stop you?" i asked her and she shrugged but i heard her mumble sumn.

"you said sumn?" i asked and she shook her head no.

i shook my head and placed my hand on her thigh again as i drove down the highway.

"you so sexy azaire...i can't explain it but you so handsome." she said and it's like that simple sentence was effecting my body bad.

my dick was starting to get hard and my face was heating up, i know for a fact my face red.

"preciate that ma." i said and i felt her grab my hand and start playing with my fingers.

"would you get your nails done wit me?" she asked.

"what you mean??" i asked turning off the highway and onto an exit.

"whatever color or designs i get on my acrylics you would get them on a few of your nails...or all of them." she said and i thought about it.

any other girl i would've said fuck no but this xylah-

"i'll do a few." i said and i could see her smile from my peripheral vision.

"really?! thank you azaire." she said and held my hand.

we finally made it to the hotel i had booked yesterday, i spent all this morning decorating it before hanging out wit taylin and benz.

"what we doing here?" she asked as i got out.

i walked out to her side and opened the door for her then helped her out,"listen i need you to trust me." i said looking in her eyes.

she nodded and grabbed the peach cobbler plates making me laugh, i grabbed it from her then grabbed her hand.

i lead her into the hotel and into the elevator,"close yo eyes." i said and she listened.

now i was starting to get nervous as the elevator started moving upwards, i chewed on my lip and held onto her hand.

i found myself smiling as she did some random lil dance.

"what is y-you doing?" i asked and she shrugged.

the elevator stopped and i lead her towards our room that was secluded and away from others.

i pulled the card from my wallet and opened the door lightly pulling her in first then closed the door.

i placed the plate on a nearby table before leading her more into the room.

"ight hollon..." i mumbled looking around the room making sure everything was good before telling her she could look.

i was behind her so i couldn't see her facial expressions but i noticed her body tensed up as she looked around the room.

"xylah..." i said catching her attention and she turned around before i could speak she jumped on me hugging me.

i instantly caught her wrapping my arms around her back as she wrapped her legs around my waist.

her face was against my shoulder as she nodded her head,"yes i'll be your girlfriend." she said into my shoulder.

"ma i ain't even g-get to do my speech." i said and she shrugged.

"i don't careee if you say it i might really start crying." she said, i walked to the bed and sat down with her in my lap.

"well...i actually wrote you a letter, i want y-you to read it please." i told her and she nodded leaning back same but stayed on my lap.

i grabbed the bag from beside the bed and handed it to her, she carefully opened it pulling out some of her favorite candies and a tennis bracelet i bought for her.

i put the bracelet on her wrist while she unfolded the letter, i watched as her eyes scanned the words and noticed they started getting glossy.

she finished it then quickly hugged me again and i heard her sniffle,"ma...don't cry y-you gonna make a nigga cry." i said and she laughed quietly.

"i'm nottt it's just...this means a lot foreal you're the first person i've ever gotten this far wit...everybody else was weird and would end up i guess tired of me or tried getting into my pants." she said.

"that's not me ma...i swear, i've liked getting to know you without doing allat other extra shit." i said and she smiled.

"well...i'll be your girlfriend and thank you for all this.." she said and i nodded.

"but azaire you did all this and you know you've planned stuff for my birthday." she said and i shrugged.

"ion care, you deserve the world. i'd give you a-anything you ask for." i told her.

"i knowww but you've done so much already." she said and pecked my lips.

"and imma be doing m-more, might as well get use to it." i said rubbing her back that was exposed.

"can we cuddle...and watch tv?" she asks nervously and i stood up before placing her on the bed.

"yeah, imma just sleep in my boxers." i said as i took off my hoodie then my t-shirt.

"can i wear your shirt?" she asked and i handed it to her.

i turned away from her as she took off her clothes,"you can look.." she said softly.

i wasn't trying to stare but soon as i turned around-

my eyes were stuck on her curves and the matching set she was wearing.

the light blue lace bra and panties complimented her skin, yet anything she wore complimented her to be honest.

"what?" she asked teasingly with my shirt in her hands.

"xylah." i said looking up at the ceiling, my dick was throbbing in my jeans right now.

i felt her hands against my chest making me look down, her titties pressed against me and i finally looked at her face that held an innocent smile.

"xylah baby please put on the shirt." i said and she shrugged stepping back.

"orrr i could just sleep in this." she said as she got onto the bed pushing some of the petals and flowers off.

man she testing me and i'm tryna hold off.

i didn't say anything as i pulled down my pants, i know for a fact my boner visible but i ignored it and dimmed the lights.

i grabbed the remote from the tv stand and sat on the end of the bed to turn it on, i heard movement behind me and felt her hands go down my chest stopping on my abs.

and she started kissing on my neck.

i thought she was innocent???

i fought back a groan that wanted to come out,"xylah-"

"please azaire..." she whispered into my ear.

# Chapter 13

♥

**X** ylah sailor summer

honestly i wasn't completely sure on what i was doing but i could tell it was working.

he blew out a breath before removing my arms and standing up, he quickly grabbed my neck before leaning down and bringing me into a tongue kiss.

it took me a few seconds but i got the hang of it, my underwear felt damp as we continued making out.

soon i was on my back and he was between my legs now attacking my neck with kisses and occasionally sucking before he leaned up and looked at me with low eyes.

"ma...i ain't got no condom." he said.

"umm i never told you but...i did get on birth control a few weeks ago." i said and he nodded.

"imma still pull out." he said before reconnecting our lips.

a few weeks ago my mom really sat down and talked to me more about the whole sex thing and she brought up birth control and i decided to get the pill...i have an alarm set everyday to take it.

when he went to pull back i sucked on his bottom lip and he groaned before completely pulling away, i watched him as he kissed down my body.

he paused at my titties and took one into his mouth while his hand reached down to rub my clit through my underwear and i was already moaning at the simple movement.

his tongue swirled around my nipple before gently biting it, he switched to the other one and i felt his finger slowly push into me.

at first it was uncomfortable but once he started moving it in and out it quickly turned to pressure,"mmm...azaire-!" i moaned loudly when he added added finger.

he lifted his head up and stared at me as he fingered me and i felt his thumb rub my clit, i bit down on my lip as i opened my legs wider for her.

he kissed me and i kissed back wrapping my arms around his neck pulling him closer to me, i moaned into his mouth as his fingers sped up.

i started moving around and he pulled back going down between my legs, he wasted no time attaching his mouth to my clit and continued moving his fingers in and out of me.

i moaned as my back arched off the bed and i gripped the sheets, his tongue flicked against my clit.

"i need you looking at me, pretty girl..." he rasped and i did my best to look at him.

i whined and propped myself up with my elbows, my stomach already felt weird as he moved his fingers in a different way and my eyes widened at the feeling.

"f-fuck wait..." i whimpered as my legs started to shake.

"unt unt let that shit go ma."

i laid back against the bed and let my body relax before i felt my juices shoot out of me, my eyes slightly started rolling back as his fingers kept moving along with his tongue.

he leaned up and i noticed his lower face wet,"damn...you do both..." he said lowly and i was kinda confused until i thought about it.

my face instantly heated up more then it already was, he hovered over me and smashed his lips against mines.

i felt his hand wrap around my neck then his tip brushed against my other lips,"you sure you wanna do this?"

i immediately nodded my head,"i'm sure..i promise azaire." i said and he nodded.

he kissed me again keeping his hand around my neck, i felt his tip against my clit it wasn't long before he started pushing himself inside of me.

and yet again it was uncomfortable for the first few seconds but he easily slid in,"fuck- azaire..." i mumbled starting to push him back.

now it was starting to hurt,"i'm sorry....you want me to stop?" he asked and i shook my head no.

i made him wait for a minute before letting him continue to push the rest of himself in.

a groan left my mouth as he held his place letting me get used to his size,"i know ma...relax." he said into my ear and i moaned as he started moving.

he started off with slow strokes placing his arms on either side of me, he was staring at my face the whole time before carefully taking my glasses off.

his thrusts sped up and my back arched off the bed and my hands went to his back, his head was now in the crook of my neck and i could her his groans.

i felt his thumb rubbing my clit and mymoans grew louder once i felt him hit a certain spot, he kept hitting that same spot and my eyes started rolling back.

"s-shit ma....you wet as fuck..." i heard him say before pressing his lips against mines.

we kissed and he slowed back down giving me hard deep strokes, i was a moaning mess.

he pulled back from the kiss and went to kissing on my neck, i could hear my wetness throughout the room along with my moaning and his occasional groans.

"you so fuckin pretty baby..." he said leaning up and staring at me.

i whimpered in response and it wasn't long before i was cumming again, i looked down between us and i could see his dick coated in white.

he randomly sped up and my legs started shaking again,"fuck..." he cursed before pulling out and nutting on the sheets.

"flip over fa me." i listened to him and got on all fours, my legs already felt weak.

"arch it."

it was the next morning and i could hear azaire moving around while i was trying to get a few more minutes of sleep.

"xylah...i k-know you up." he said and tapped my thigh.

i groaned and pulled the cover over my head,"you gotta put clothes on." he said.

i slowly sat up and groaned at the soreness between my legs, i carefully walked to the bathroom and quickly did what i needed.

i just put back on the clothes i had yesterday, i'd worry about showering when i get home.

when i came back out i seen he had whatever in a trash bag then handed me my gift bag. while he went to check out i went ahead to his car and got in the passenger seat leaning my seat back.

i checked my phone since i hadn't been on it since we left the restaurant.

sage: xylahhh!! you ready for your birthday

ayani: righttt it's almost here bitch we turning up for yo day

-am i excited? yeahh a lil bit i think i wanna drink a lil

sage: SAY NO MO SAY NO MO

ayani: you done got her alcoholic ass happy

sage: you ever pause and think maybe the liquor addicted to me

-guys should i get long or short nails my appointment in a few days

sage: long

ayani emphasized 'long'

-bet bet bet

ayani: what colors you want us to wear?

-umm i guess white would be fine

sage: okay okay, i'm so ready to see how you're gonna lookkk

ayani: sameeee know she finna look bad asf

-would y'all wanna come over before we all go out?

ayani: yesss we can get ready together if you want

-yeah that would be fun, y'all can meet my pet pig

sage: pet pig??? is it nice?

-she and yesall she do is sleep and eat fr

azaire got in the car and i put my phone up as he buckled up,"you wanna get sumn to eat?" he asked then leaned over the console and pecked my lips.

"yeah.." i said smiling and he nodded as he started the car.

as he drove i found myself dozing off, somehow i was still tired from last night.

"xylah...xylah get up." he said and i opened my eyes seeing we were in front of my house.

"damn...i slept the whole time?" i asked and he nodded.

"you got some h-hickeys on yo neck..." he said and i used my camera to look at them.

"lemme take your hoodie." i said and he took it off and handed it to me.

i put it on and fixed it to where it would cover my neck more,"you wanna come inside and eat?" i suggested and he nodded.

my parents and siblings were home, we got out and walked to the front door.

i unlocked the door and made my way to my room,"we can take a shower before we eat..." i said and he nodded.

"together?" he asked with a smirk and i rolled my eyes.

"i guess- don't try anything i'm sore." i pouted and he laughed pecking my lips.

"my bad, you w-were the one saying 'moreee' 'go deeperrr'." he mocked me and i playfully pushed him away from me while laughing.

# Chapter 14

♥

**A** zaire kade carmine

i groaned as my phone started ringing, i swear i just went to sleep 15 minutes ago....

it was the day before xylah's birthday and last night i spent i don't know how long out doing drop offs and drills.

i got extra money just in case, then i had spent the day making sure everything was in place for her day...i wasn't trying to do things last minute.

my eyes automatically squint as i try to read the name across my bright phone screen,"hello?" i rasped out rubbing my eyes.

"yo..azaire, i think you needa come over.." i heard namari's voice and muffled voices and crying in the background.

"what's going on?" i asked as i quickly sat up.

"i don't exactly know how much xylah told you about her autism, but she has these moments where she can have episodes or fits— and right now i feel like she really needs you.." she said and i was putting on clothes as she spoke.

"shit- i've been trying to m-make sure everything straight for her birthday, i'll admit i haven't spent as much t-time with her but i still check in on her w-when i can." i quickly explained as i looked for my car keys.

"don't think the episode is specifically just about you, it's other things she doesn't always talk about." she said.

"alright i'm finna be on the way." i said before hanging up.

matiyah opened the door for me,"she's in her bedroom...be careful with certain things you say right now."

i nodded and walked down the hall, i could hear her sniffles once i got to her door.

i knocked on her door instead of just walking in, i didn't get a response and i slowly opened her bedroom door.

i looked around her room and it was slightly messy, she was balled up against the wall hugging herself and clawing at her arms.

i shrugged off my jacket and sat down in front of her,"pretty girl..."

once i spoke her eyes snapped to mine, they were bloodshot and puffy. her face red and stained with tears.

"what's wrong ma?" i asked softly and she whimpered before holding her arms out.

i quickly took her into my lap,"you w-wanna talk about it?" i asked and she quickly shook her head no hanging onto me as if i would disappear.

"you know i gotchu, right?" i asked her and she nodded.

i used my shirt to wipe her face, once i was done she looked up at me before speaking,"kiss..." she mumbled.

a small smile came on my face and i leaned down pecking her lips, nose, and forehead.

i got up and kept her in my arms and walked over to her bed placing her on it,"sorry..." she mumbled.

"for what? you d-didn't do anything baby." i told her as i slipped off my t-shirt.

"my room...it's a mess, and i know- namari called you over." she said as she rubbed her eyes.

"right now my room looks worse, and i'll drop w-whatever i'm doing to be with you." i said taking off my shoes then i laid down and pulled her on top of me.

she laid her head on my chest and i rubbed her back as i felt her hand tracing my arm tattoos.

"i was...i don't know- i'm still kinda scared i guess...all this is new to me azaire. friendships, relationships, sex, and actually being out." she vented and i nodded.

"did i move too fa-"

"no it's not that, i was ready it's just what if you leave me."

my face immediately frowned up,"why w-would you think that?" i asked and she sighed.

"i don't know....like you haven't showed me any signs of you cheating or anything, but what if you're good at hiding it or one day you get tired of me.."

"xylah- look at me." i said and she lifted her head from my chest looking at me with glossy eyes.

"i'm not going nowhere...i promise you that. when i asked you to be my girlfriend it was because..i feel at home with you...i c-can tell you anything and you don't judge me. you're my comfort place whenever i need an escape f-from my mind. i'd never get bored of you. i lo—" i stopped myself.

"i feel the same with you...i do tend to overthink and be in my head a lot and i feel at some point it'll become too much for you..." she mumbled rubbing my beard hair.

"it won't...you can tell me whatever is on yo mind..." i said before yawning.

"you're tired?" she asked and i shook my head no.

"your eyes are halfway closed- and you don't smell like weed so?" she said and i laughed.

"i'm good...you needa go to sleep. you got all y-your appointments in a few hours." i said.

"take a nap with me." she said and i nodded.

i woke up to the sound of xylah's shower, i looked around her room and saw she must've cleaned up when she got up.

i had a slight headache, i knew it was from lack of sleeping but i'll just take another nap later.

i sat up and checked my phone seeing my dad called so i called him back,"son where the hell yo black ass at?!"

"dad, we share locations." i said shaking my head.

"no we- oh....that's xylah house?" he asked and i hummed in response.

"i left early this morning b-because she needed me." i explained.

"alright...next time let me or your mom know. you gonna be staying with her today?" he asked.

"yeah i should be back by tonight tho..." i said and her shower door opened.

she walked out with a towel wrapped around her, she looked over at me and smiled before sitting on my lap.

"okay, be safe. i love you."

"i love you too." i said before hanging up.

"who was that?" she asked and i showed her my call log.

"ohh...you get any good sleep?" she asked and i nodded before pecking her lips.

i swear to God i could kiss her lips all fuckin day.

"what about you?" she nodded smiling at me.

"what?" i asked and she shook her head before hugging me.

"baby, you still got t-this towel on you..." i said noticing it was starting to fall.

"can you come with me to my appointments today, please?" she asked and i nodded.

"buttt we're taking my car." she said.

"that's fine, you wanna drive or me?" i asked her and she shrugged getting up.

"we can switch back and forth...can you put this lotion on my back?" she asked.

i grabbed the bottle from her dresser and she turned around letting her towel fall down to her waist, i squeezed some in my hand then rubbed the lotion on her back.

the cocoa scent instantly filled the room, once i was done i allowed her to finish getting ready.

"can you order us some mcdonald's?" she asked as she pulled up her flared leggings.

"what you want ma?"

"sausage biscuit and an iced caramel macchiato with extra caramel please." she said and i went to doordash and started the order.

i got the same as her except with orange juice then decided to go pick it up,"bae." she said making me turn towards her and i looked over her outfit.

she had on a long sleeve grey crop top with matching flared leggings and black crocs on. she still had on her bonnet so i took it as she was wearing it out.

"baeee." i snapped out my trance and paid attention.

"yes ma?"

"i said have you been working out more? your abs look more defined." she said and it made me look down at my stomach.

"i've found some more workouts that's more hardcore, b-but i'm finna take a break for a few days." i said and she nodded.

i put back on my shirt and jacket then laced up my air forces.

we made it outside to her car and i was driving first, i opened the car door for her then closed it once she was inside.

i got in the drivers seat and started the car as she connected her phone to the aux.

Girl if I told you I love youThat doesn't mean that I don't care, ooohAnd when I tell you I need youDon't you think that I'll never be there, ooooh

played as she placed her phone down and leaned back in her seat, i pulled out the driveway then placed my hands in hers as i drove with the other.

"azaire..." she spoke once i pulled into mcdonald's parking lot.

"yeah ma?"

she grabbed my chin pulling me closer to her before kissing my lips, i kissed her back and felt her tongue against my lips.

i opened my mouth and her tongue quickly invaded my mouth, i did the same back gripping her neck hearing a small moan leaving her lips.

i pulled back cause the last thing i was tryna do was fuck her in a mcdonald's parking lot.

"i love you." she said and a smile stretched across my face.

"i love you more pretty." i said and pecked her lips one last time.

"imma get the food real quick." i told her and she nodded getting on her phone.

# Chapter 15

♥

Xylah sailor summer

"wake up!" i heard making me groan as i rolled over.

"babygirlllll!!!! it's yo birthday fuck nigga." i finally pulled my cover from over my face and saw namari standing there with ballon's and gift bags making me smile.

"a happy birthday would've been fine." i said rubbing my eyes and she shrugged.

"ehh yo mama and brothers will do allat, hmm open them." she said handing me the bags and tied the balloons to my bed post.

"where's coco?" i asked and she pointed towards my window basically saying outside.

i nodded and started going through the bags, each bag making me smile more and more. she had gotten me a micheal kors bag, different charms for my pandora bracelet, a bag full of bath and body work perfumes, and finally money.

"thank youuu." i said getting up and hugged her.

"you're welcome princess, get ready so you can open the gifts your mama bought you...i already sold the lingerie she tried to get you." she said and my jaw dropped.

"really?" i asked and she shrugged.

"i don't know she kinda forced me to put some back." she said before walking out my bedroom.

i shook my head before quickly grabbing my phone to check my notifications.

azaire: happy birthday ma, i can't wait to see you and do everything i got planned just know you staying wit me the whole weekend at an airbnb wit the gang. i love yo pretty ass

-i love you moree thank youuu, i can't wait are you coming to the restaurant wit my family?

next i checked the group chat.

sage: AHHH BITCH ITS YO BIRTHDAYYY

ayani: HAPPY BIRTHDAYYY i'm ready asf for tonighttttt

-thank youuu and i am TOOO, y'all got the bottles right?

sage: girl we got luna, casa, patron, and pink whitney

ayani: now listen we not letting you get crazy drunk plus azaire ass probably gonna be tryna babysit

-i'll have him taking shots wit me cause i'm tryna be tore up

sage: ME AND SCOOB TOE UP ALREADY!!

i laughed and walked to my bathroom to take a quick shower, once i was done i took off my scarf and carefully combed my hair.

i had a sew in and closure in, the hair had loose curls with layers and came down my back.

my nails were coffin shaped, orange french tip nails that were xl. azaire ended up getting his nails done with me, clear coat and a random orange X on his right pinky finger.

yeahhh my initial.

i put on the black lace bodysuit i had then my black leather pants, i fixed my lash extensions then put on a lil bit of concealer.

i put on my black heels and took one final look at everything, once i was happy with how i looked i grabbed my phone then went to the living room where my brothers and mama was at.

"happy birthday my loveee! open these then we can get going." my mama said and i nodded as my brothers ran to hug me.

i hugged my aunt nalani as i looked around at the reserved area that was for me.

"happy birthday girl, you getting big and shit." she said making me laugh.

"mhmm...that boyfriend of yours coming?" uncle rome asked me and i slick rolled my eyes.

"businessss." mama said waving him off then she showed me where i was sitting at.

i sat down and started watching azaire's location, he was pulling into the parking lot.

azaire: sumn telling me you watching my location

azaire: should i bring the stuff i bought you in?

-what did you get me

azaire:

you loved an image

-yessss thank youuuu sm

azaire: you're welcome pretty i'm finna come in

"mama azaire finna walk in." i said and that made rome, kai, and my grandparents perk up immediately.

namari laughed before speaking,"y'all acting just like me when i first heard about dude." she shook her head.

i looked towards the entrance and saw him walk in and was looking around until a waitress walked up to him.

i couldn't make out the conversation but he look annoyed, it was funny he always had a mean look on his face when talking to people.

he made eye contact with me instantly smiling and started walking my way.

"and don't y'all dare act like hooligans." nalani said to the boys and i laughed some getting up.

i hugged him once he was close enough and he sat the cake and pandora bag down before hugging me back.

"you look pretty ma." he said looking over my outfit then handed me the flowers.

i took the time to look at what he was wearing, light green cargo pants with a white t-shirt and a black sweater that has a green design on it with white and black dunks. he also had on a few chains and stud earrings in his ears.

"thank you- hollon this alot of people to introduce lowkey..." i mumbled.

after everybody introducing theirselves and azaire doing the same back we finally we're able to start ordering.

"you think this good?" i asked azaire as he sat his phone down.

he looked at the menu where i was pointing at,"ion know...m-maybe. i was just gonna get some ribs." he said and i nodded.

"i lowkey want some crab cakes.." i mumbled.

"then-" he was cut off by the same waitress from earlier.

"and what can i get you to drink." she asked him but the way she asked....

azaire kept his eyes down on the menu before speaking,"sprite.." he said wrapping his arm around me.

"and for you birthday girl?" she asked and the look on her face had dropped some seeing azaire's arm.

"sweet tea." i said and azaire pulled my chair closer to his.

once she got everyone's drink she left,"my bad if you ain't wanna be t-this close...she was staring at me too hard." he said.

"it's fine." i said laying my head on his shoulder.

"can i open it?" i asked looking at the pandora bag.

"go ahead."

i excitedly grabbed it and pulled out the small box from inside, he held the bag for me while i opened the box and my mouth dropped.

"you remembered!" i said and he smiled at me as i pulled the ring out.

"i know you not really a huge fan of b-big and flashy stuff...so it's simple but it'll still be shiny." he said grabbing my hand and slipped the ring onto my finger.

"aweee it's so pretty- hold it in the light so i can get a picture." mama said and i laughed doing as she said.

"azaire lean in closer." she told him.

"he close enough." namari said raising her eyebrow.

"let them be." aunt nalani said.

once mama got the picture everyone went back to their own convo, "bae..." i mumbled and he hummed.

"what we doing this weekend??" i asked and he looked at me.

"you better be a morning person cause i got stuff planned for the whole day tomorrow, tonight tho we just gonna chill at the house with the gang." he said.

"okay." i said sitting up as our drinks and food came out.

"bae i can get some of your ribs.." i mumbled and he gave me a side eye before pushing his plate over.

# Chapter 16

♥

Xylah sailor summer

"you didn't say it was gonna be near the beachhh! look at the view." i said walking onto the balcony.

the airbnb was two stories, downstairs had a kitchen, living room, half a bathroom and a patio outside.

upstairs had 3 bedrooms with a bathroom in two and one in the hallway, and i'm pretty sure it's a balcony for each other room but ours was the biggest.

he also had the room decorated before we got here, it was balloons and pictures of us on the bed.

"i didn't wanna spoil everything ma...." azaire said as he sat on the bed and took off his hoodie.

"i'm surprised yo ass didn't get c-cold with what you wearing." he said and i sat on his lap.

"did you post me?" i asked him and he nodded handing me his phone.

zaireee_ 2m
send message
i smiled and reposted it to my story since he at me.

"thank you so much." i said straddling his lap and hugged him.

"bae later on...when we drink and stuff can we you know..." i mumbled rubbing his face and he smiled at me.

"definitely." he said making me laugh.

he hugged me back while leaning down onto the bed, we all had went out to eat and now everyone was settling in their rooms.

on the way here azaire and i smoked a blunt so i was a tad bit high,"you gonna drink everything with me?" i asked him and he nodded staring at me.

"what you finna change into f-for tonight?" he asked me and i got up to find my bag.

"probably these shorts and a black sports bra." i said pulling out my hello kitty pajama shorts.

"ight, throw me a pair of my sweats." he said and i went into his bag pulling out the first pair of sweats i felt.

grey? unt unt.

i threw him a black pair then carefully took off my dress leaving me in my underwear, just as i was about to put on my shorts-

i felt azaire pull me back into his lap, immediately i felt his bugle against my ass.

"azaire-"

"wassup baby?" he said as one of his hands went to my chest and the other between my leg.

"you okay wit me doing this?" he asked and once i nodded his hand immediately went to rub my clit under my underwear.

my legs opened wider and i moaned as he went to my neck and started kissing my neck while massaging my breast.

"lay on yo back." he said and i got up from his lap to the bed.

he stood up and pulled me to the edge of the bed by my legs, he took off my underwear and my eyes went to the bulge in his pants.

he clearly had other plans as he kneeled down and attached his mouth to my clit, i bit down on my lip cause i have no idea how thin these walls are.

that plan quickly failed when two of his fingers entered me and started moving at a fast pace, my mouth fell open and the only thing heard was my wetness and my quiet moans.

what i hope we're quiet.

right as i came, he removed his fingers and fully stood up. i sat up and grabbed his arms pulling him down on top of me.

he flipped us over and i was sitting right on his covered bulge, i lifted up and allowed him to pull down his boxers before connecting our lips.

i felt him moving before he broke the kiss and tapped my thigh,"lean up..." he said and i noticed a condom in his hand.

once he placed it on he threw the wrapper to the floor then pushed me down onto his dick, i immediately felt him stretching me out all over again.

"shit....you tight as fuck..." he groaned slamming me down onto him.

i moaned loudly once i started bouncing faster on his dick, i heard a few moans escape his lips as he placed his hands on my hips.

one of his hands reached to grip my neck while the other firmly held my waist as he thrusted upwards immediately hitting my spot, i was basically melting in his hold.

freak hoe by future was currently blasting in the living room while we were drinking.

"come on birthday girlll, shot o clock." sage sung holding up the bottle of casamigos that was halfway gone.

honestly we all had done a shared amount on drinking not only that but the patron and pink whitney too.

i lazily stood up from azaire's lap and sage walked over to pour the drink in my mouth while ayani recorded on her phone.

once a good amount was in my mouth she moved the bottle and allowed me to swallow what was in my mouth, the alcohol had a minimal burn now since i was starting to get use to the taste.

the first shot i took of anything i needed a chaser immediately after.

Freak hoes, freak hoesBounce that ass make your knees touch your elbowsFreak hoes, freak hoes

"bow bow!!" ayani hyped me up as i bent over and twerked.

i felt an arm around my waist and immediately knew it was azaire, he was behind me feeling on my ass.

"alrighttt you know how to make that booty moveeee!" sage said looking at me surprised.

as the night went on, we continued drinking, playing games, and a smallll bit of smoking.

i sat on the couch with ayani and sage while the boys continued played uno and scrolled on instagram.

my story 5h

send message

sagebabyy 9h

send message

2h

send message

yourstruly_ayanii 12h

45m
send message

"y'all wanna finish this??" ayani asked holding up a bottle of don julio that was almost gone.

it was funny cause all of our eyes look weak,"yuppp." sage dragged out holding her cup up.

ayani poured some into her cup then held the bottle towards me, i took the bottle and drunk the rest that was in there.

this shit starting to taste like water...

i looked over azaire and he had low eyes and was laughing with the boys as taylin passed him the blunt, he took a long hit and threw down a +2 making the boys smack their lips.

azaire looked at me and i just stared back at him, he walked off towards the stairs first.

i waited a few minutes before yawning and stretching,"damn yo ass tired already?" ayani asked and i nodded.

"i think all the liquor starting to hit me..." i said rubbing my eyes and i saw sage smirk at me.

"what?" i asked and she shook her head laughing.

"nun...gone head wit yo boo." she said waving me off and ayani laughed.

"girl don't get pregnant on this trip." ayani said and i gave her a thumbs up before getting up.

i barely made my way up the stairs and into the bedroom, when i closed the door i made sure it was locked.

when i looked around the room i could see the balcony door open and heard turn on the lights by future playing, i walked outside and he was looking over the balcony.

i carefully touched his back and he turned around to face me,"yo ass was in t-there undressing me wit yo eyes." he said and i laughed.

"maybe...maybe not..." i said as i dragged my hand down his body to his waist band tucking my hand inside his boxers.

he stared down at me and licked his lips while i gently grabbed his dick and slowly started stroking him, he was already hard.

he grabbed my chin and leaned down to kiss me while i continued my hand movements, i could hear his breathing change up and felt his body moving.

he moaned into my mouth and that made me even wetter, he broke the kiss and leaned his head back and a groan left his mouth as i felt his dick twitch in my hands.

i pulled my hand out of his boxers seeing some of his nut on my hand, i licked it off and he watched me with lust in his eyes.

he changed our positions to where i was bent over the balcony and his body was pressed against mines.

"baby...you trust me?" he asked and i nodded.

most people back down in a moment like this but...i wanted it..badly.

"ma..."

"yes azaire i do." i said and i felt his hands pull my shorts down to my knees and i felt his dick press against my clit.

i'm glad these houses have a lot of space between them.

once he pushed himself in my legs turned to jelly, he held his hands tightly on my waste and i arched my back against him.

he was moving slow but hitting deep every stroke, i was a moaning mess and felt like i was gonna explode. he held my hair wrapped around his hand pulling me up against his chest.

i heard him groaning into my ear while i bit on my lip feeling myself close to cumming already,"gone head and cum fa me pretty..." he rasped in my ear.

his voice did it for me- almost immediately i came undone feeling my legs buckle as he held me up.

i heard him curse before pulling out and nutting on my back,"sh it...c'mere." he said turning me around and kissing my lips.

the kiss was sloppy and heated, he grabbed my thighs and i jumped on him wrapping my legs around his waist.

he walked back inside and to the bed laying me down, he kissed down my neck and chest before walking to the balcony to close and lock the door.

i tried to get up and my legs felt wobbly but i made my way to the bathroom and he followed as i turned the water all the way to hot.

"b-bae i don't wanna be a seafood boil." he said and i rolled my eyes.

"it's not even that hot bae." i said and he groaned walking up behind me and wrapped his arms around me.

he was still semi hard...

"just a shower azaire." i said and he laughed kissing my neck.

"i hear you." he said and he smacked my ass hard.

"i hope you not sore tomorrow..." he mumbled and i shook my head.

# Chapter 17

♥

**Xylah sailor summer**

so today we had went zip lining, to an arcade, and atv riding on a trail nearby, and i'll admit it's been fun.

waking up wasn't cause my head was surely pounding hard as fuck, i took medicine and ate and was wearing sunglasses for half the day but my headache has died down.

"aye is y'all niggas hungry yet?" taylin asked as we all got into the golf carts.

"my stomach touching my damn back." ayani said and we all laughed.

"it's gonna be food b-back at the place when we get there." azaire said and off they went speeding down the street.

azaire and i in one cart, sage and taylin in one, then ayani and benz.

once we made it back to the house everyone went to their own rooms first,"after we eat we should wait then go to the beach." i suggested and he nodded.

"yeah we can do that." he said as he took off his t-shirt then his pants.

i took off biker shorts and top i had on then changed into one of my bikinis.

i text the girls and told them the plans then i looked in the mirror and took a picture before posting it.

once i looked back up i saw azaire had on his swimming shorts and was staring at me.

"what??" i asked and he shook his head.

"you just beautiful as hell." he said grabbing my hand and pulled me into his lap.

i sat in his lap and pecked his lips,"thank you baby...you look so handsome." i said and he smiled at me before nuzzling his face between my breast.

i shook my head and got on my phone.

my story 3h

send message

2m

send message

zaireee_ 2h

send message

"baeee it was animals out there." i said and he shrugged not moving his head.

"come on so we can eat, i just h-heard your stomach growl." he said finally moving his head and i laughed.

i was about to get up but he picked me up and walked us out the room,"finally thought y'all was fuckin again." benz said and i immediately felt my face heat up.

"business, get you some." azaire said sitting down and sat me in his lap.

"he just mad he ain't got nun on this trip." sage said laying her head on taylin shoulders before quickly sitting up cause he flinched.

"i think i got sunburned." taylin said and i noticed he did have some tan lines and his skin was a tad bit red.

"i told yo light bright ass to wear the damn sunscreen." sage said shaking her head.

i started eating the hot wings from the plate with my name on it while azaire ate his,"it's this water park by us, i was wondering if y'all wanna go there first then the beach." ayani said and i nodded.

"we can, that way we won't be tracking sand back to the water park and stuff...and when we leave the beach we can come straight back to the house." i said and wiped my mouth.

"they asses go to sleep any kind of way..." i heard as i started waking up.

"it's called being in love you should try it sometimes." i heard benz voice followed my quiet laughter.

"i know yo hoe ass ain't talking..." ayani said then i heard footsteps disappearing.

i slowly opened my eyes and saw we were outside on the patio.

we went to the water park and beach, and once i got back i was TIRED. i don't understand how but water will tire the fuck out of you.

azaire and i took a shower then got dressed to come and sit on the patio with everyone and just talk and smoke some.

during that we had to fall asleep.

taylin and sage were sitting in a chair together, benz was sitting on the couch and ayani came back with water bottles.

then i realized how me and azaire were laying which was lowkey funny. i swear we lay any way as long as we're touching.

i didn't move much but grabbed a bottle from ayani,"sleep good?" she asked and i nodded.

that nap HIT.

"yeah- how long was i out?" i asked.

"about 4 hours, he look like he finna be out for 5." benz said and i looked at azaire who was still knocked out completely.

"you gotta be his melatonin or sumn, cause i ain't never seen him knock out so easily." sage said shaking her head.

right as i tried untangling our bodies, azaire started waking up turning his head to face me.

"what is you doing?" he asked with a mug.

"moving-"

"stop, c'mere." he mumbled pulling me back and closed his eyes again.

"oh yeah his ass love sick." taylin said laughing.

azaire lazily held up his arm and flipped them off.

"i'll send you the picture boo." ayani said and my phone went off.

i grabbed my phone and shook my head.

ayani:

you loved an image

"tryna get like y'all foreal." benz said and i shook my head as i scrolled on my phone.

mama: you enjoying your trip??

-yes ma'am, have you been looking at my insta story?

mama: yes i have y'all are so adorable together, just don't come back pregnant

-.....mama

mama: i'm just sayinggg tell azaire i said hey

-he sleep

mama: you got that nyquil pussy???

-GOODBYE

"what the hell..." i mumbled exiting out the text thread.

i love being close with my parents but sometimes they kill me wit certain things they say.

namari:do you want me to bathe this pig?

-no i can do it when i get back tomorrow, make sure she gets them apple slices in the fridge tho

namari: ight what all you been doing

-going out, eating

namari: mhm better not be pregnant

-you and mama both finna get blocked

namari: and imma whoop yo ass

-you've never whooped any of us

namari: ntm now, enjoy the rest of the trip i love you

-i love you too

i sighed as i looked up at the sky, the sun was setting fast as hell to be honest.

"ouuu y'all wanna make s'mores?" sage asked.

"yeah we can actually make a lil fire in this pit." ayani said and i nodded.

"sounds good- if i can get up." i said as i tried to move my legs but azaire reached up and grabbed me before i could get far.

"baeee imma get the chocolate and stuff so we can have s'mores." i whined.

he smacked his lips but let me go, i got up and went inside with sage and ayani.

"you've been enjoying your birthday trip?" ayani asked and i nodded.

"a lot actually...thanks for coming along." i said to them and they smiled.

"of course, you apart of the group now. we love having another girl around. " sage said as she grabbed the crackers.

i grabbed the chocolate and ayani grabbed the marshmallows,"nowww when one of y'all gonna have a baby for the gang?" i asked them.

"girl you better be asking sage and taylin." ayani said as we walked back outside.

"uhhh i wanna be the rich auntie with no kids, why can't one of y'all do it?" sage asked.

"wellll one she just turned 17, two i ain't got nobody to make a baby daddy. niggas be weird as fuck..." ayani said sitting down.

the boys had started a fire and azaire was finally sitting up, i sat on his lap and grabbed the sticks that was beside him.

sage had a plate that held the crackers and what not while we passed around sticks.

"ma..." i heard azaire whisper and i turned around to face him moving my marshmallow from the fire.

"hmm?" i hummed as his eyes roamed my face.

"i just wanna tell you, you m-mean the world to me. i love you so fuckin much ion think i've ever felt this way before about anyone. i never wanna lose you..." he said and i smiled before kissing his lips.

"i love you more azaire. i promise i'm here for the good and bad..." i said holding out my pinky.

he laughed but locked his with mines.

"forever?" i asked.

"forever..."he said and pecked my lips.

# Chapter 18

♥

**Azaire kade carmine**

i huffed as i walked out my therapists office to my car.

xylah:babbyyyyy

i smiled seeing her text and i responded once i got in the car.

-heyy pretty girl

xylah: can you come get me

- yeah whats wrong

xylah: my period came on and everybody pissing me off

-ight i'm leaving therapy, i'll be there in 30

xylah loved 'ight i'm leaving therapy, i'll be there in 30'

xylah: hurry up please

-i am ma, i love you

-where tf my emoji at

-I LOVE YOU

xylah:I LOVE YOU MORE

i shook my head going to the starbucks app xylah downloaded on my phone, i ordered her favorite drink along with a cake pop before going to the nearest walgreens.

i parked outside xylah's house and she slowly walked to the car with a bag over her shoulder.

she had on sweatpants and an oversized sweater, on her head was the custom bonnet i bought her.

she made it in the car and i watched her mug turn into a smile at the starbucks and flowers in the seat,"bae imma cry." she pouted and i laughed.

"yo emotional ass....i g-got you some snacks in the back." i told her and she nodded getting situated and started drinking her starbucks.

"you want some?" she asked holding the cup towards me and i shook my head no.

as i drove back home she held my right hand, occasionally stopping just to play with my fingers.

once we got to my house i realized she had fell asleep, i got out grabbing her bags then gently shaked her.

she groaned in response,"c'mere ma." i said and she wrapped her arms around my neck as i picked her up.

her legs wrapped around my waist as i walked to my house, both my parents were gone right now but they'll be back by tonight.

i made it to my room sitting her bags on the floor then laid her down on my bed, i took off my t-shirt and pants leaving me in my boxers.

"bae- help." xylah said and i looked over at her to see her struggling to take off the sweater.

i couldn't help but laugh, i got on the bed and helped her pull it over hear head leaving her in a sports bra.

"azaire stop staring at them." she mumbled pulling the cover over her.

"my bad....they just be sitting pretty." i said and she rolled her eyes before grabbing my arm and pulling me closer to her.

"can you take a nap with me?" she asked with a pout.

"yeah..." i mumbled getting in bed beside her.

she snuggled close to me putting her head in the crook of my neck while i rubbed her back,"azaire..." she mumbled and i hummed in response.

"i know i don't say it a lot but i'm really glad your my first...i love everything about you.." she said before yawning.

i found myself smiling and kissed her forehead before speaking,"i love e-everything about you too...i love you don't judge me for nun i do. you're there whenever i need you and i appreciate you for that. you don't care about the shit i can get you either..and honestly that's a first." i said and she moved closer to me if possible.

"you love me for who i am...and i'll forever be grateful for that." i told her.

"bae...you keep talking like that imma end up sucking yo dick..." she mumbled and i laughed.

"nah we taking a nap remember." i said.

"i'll do it befo...." she stopped talking making me realize she had fell asleep.

i slowly woke up and saw xylah walking into my room with chips,candy, and my moms coffee mug.

now she had on one of my hoodies and shorts, both them looking big as hell on her.

"xylah??" i rasped and she jumped looking at me.

"your mom home....and she made me tea." she said and i shook my head sitting up and yawning.

she sat on my gaming chair and i noticed the tv had spongebob playing,"h-how long you've been up?"

"ummm a hour...you looked like you were sleeping good so i didn't wanna wake you up..." she said and i nodded.

"bae i gotta tell you umm the other night this girl text me asking bout you..." she said and i scrunched up my face.

"who?"

"i don't know her but i can send you her page...she said y'all slept together recently or sumn...i know y'all haven't but i just found it weird."

"why you didn't tell me when it happened?" i asked grabbing her phone and put in her passcode.

"because- i didn't care to be honest. i know you aren't cheating unless...." she mumbled raising an eyebrow at me.

"i'm not xylah, i put that shit on my life." i said scrolling on instagram until i saw it-

"on my fuckin mama, i'll kill that bitch." i blurted feeling myself get mad.

"umm...azaire..." xylah mumbled turning the chair to look towards me.

"my bad- she's m-my ex....her dumbass got me setup then had the nerve to say she was pregnant by me. t-then said she got an abortion cause it wasn't mine." i quickly explained.

xylah's eyes widened,"oh..." she mumbled opening the bag of chips.

"ignore her..and i'm blocking her from yo shit...already gonna kill ha ass on the spot..." i mumbled the last part.

"okay i'm sorry i brought it up.." she said getting up and walked to me.

"i'm glad you t-told me...." i said shaking my head and she put the chips down before she started rubbing my face.

"calm down..." she mumbled leaning forward and pecked my lips.

"i am-"

"no you're not...your face immediately started turning red and you breathing faster then normal." she said and i huffed.

"my b-bad. i really forgot about the bitch existence until just now." i said leaning my head against her chest.

"you want me to fight her?"

"xylah...hell nah cause soon as her fist c-connect wit yo face im shooting everybody. and i'll be damned she try and jump yo ass." i said looking up at her and she sat down on my lap.

"chip?" she mumbled holding a salt and vinegar chip towards my mouth.

i let her feed it to me as she continued munching on the rest.

"can we go to sage and taylin's apartment this weekend?" she asked and i nodded.

"of course ma." i said and she nodded.

"my period will be off by the weekend...you should take me to the trap wit you one day." she smiled and i shook my head.

"if i do, y-you not staying for long. ion want you around allat shit." i said putting my hand underneath my hoodie and rubbing her stomach.

she groaned putting the chips down and grabbed the coffee mug taking a sip,"you and this tea really helping my cramps." she said laying her head on my shoulder.

"i'm glad i can help baby." i said kissing her forehead.

# Chapter 19

♥

Xylah sailor summer

"xylahhh yo man here." i heard sage say while rubbing my back.

i groaned as i started waking up,"i wanna sleep longer..." i mumbled and she laughed.

"i'll let him know boo." she said then walked back out the room.

azaire had been out with the guys doing whatever street shit, so i came to sage and taylins apartment.

sage and ayani were here, we had went out to eat and when we came back i went straight to sleep.

i heard the bedroom door open,"ma..."

i ignored him turning on my side,"baby!" he said loudly then i felt the bed dip and he pulled me on his lap.

"you had fun?" i asked wrapping my arms around his neck.

"not really..." he said and i looked up at his face seeing his eyes were low and red.

"you've been smoking a lot lately..." i mumbled.

"i know...d-does it bother you?" he asked and i shrugged.

"i mean...i've just saying i've noticed you've been doing it more that's all." i said and and he stood up keeping me in his arms.

we joined everybody else in the living room me in his lap,"ahh—shit sage damn." taylin said and i noticed sage cleaning a bad cut on his arm.

"shut the fuck up..." she snapped continuing what she was doing.

i looked away and back at azaire who seemed zoned out and in his own world.

"the twins been asking about you." i said and he stared at me.

"when you go home i'll come with you and see em...but before that i-i wanna take you on a date.." he said rubbing my back and i smiled.

"really? where?" i asked.

"you'll see when we get there...you don't have to go change or anything either." he said and i nodded.

"aye you going back on the block tonight?" benz asked azaire.

azaire shook his head no,"nah imma be wit xylah." he said.

azaire put his attention back on me,"how yo grades been looking?"

"i got all a's- except i got a d in history." i frowned.

"have you been asking for help?" he asked me and i shook my head no.

"because...people already steadily ask if i understand things because im autistic so when i actually need help it's like..irritating to ask." i explained and he nodded.

"you could've asked me and i would've helped you ma...you know this." he said and i sighed.

"before we go out..imma help you, come on." he said tapping my thigh and i got up.

"we'll see y'all later."

"hand me the wipes." azaire said and i handed him the cleaning wipes.

i watched as he cleaned off his hands then did the same to mines.

we were at a reserved area that had a clear overview of the city. he had bought art supplies and a basket full of different snacks for us.

we already ate, and just finished painting. before coming here we did stop by my house where he talked to my parents and siblings. then he helped me on some of my history work.

"thank you for earlier...i appreciate it." i told him as he stood up.

"it's no p-problem prettygirl." he said holding his hand out and helping me up.

i grabbed the basket while he grabbed the blanket from the ground, he opened his trunk and put the blanket in along with the basket.

he placed the paintings on a trash bag in the backseat on the floor then opened the passenger door for me to get in then got in the drivers seat.

"you had fun today?" he asked me and i nodded.

"yeah i did." i said as he connected his phone to his aux and leaned his seat back.

oh, you got power, superpowersdo you even know how to wield them?all God's children are specialbut not like you, no, not like you

super powers by daniel caesar played lowly as i stared at him.

"that's good...i wanted to do sumn fa you..let you k-know i'm really in love wit yo ass xylah. i swear to God mane. i ain't never think i'd find somebody like you baby." he said staring at me.

i found myself smiling and was staring right back at him,"i love you so much." i told him leaned over and pecked his lips.

i went to pull back and he grabbed my neck kissing me again, i crawled over the console and into his lap.

"hollon..." he rasped pulling back and i watched him take his gun and place it on the passenger seat.

he leaned up taking off his hoodie and t-shirt then pulled me against his chest and we started making out again.

his hands went to my waist then inside my leggings, one hand on my butt the other between my legs rubbing my clit.

i moaned into his mouth as his fingers slid inside of me moving at a slow pace then he started kissing my neck.

"baby..." i whimpered and he hummed in response moving his fingers faster.

i put my face in the crook of his neck, lightly biting it. he pulled my leggings down and leaned me back against the wheel.

"you so fuckin pretty ma..." he rasped staring in my eyes as his fingers moved in and out of me at a fast pace.

i whined feeling myself start to squirt already, he only moved his fingers faster and held a grip on my neck.

"backseat." was all he said once he moved his fingers from me.

i crawled in the back and took my leggings all the way off along with my shirt keeping my bra on.

the back door opened and azaire got in closing it behind him,"lay on yo back." he told me as he took off his shorts.

once i laid back comfortably i felt his mouth attach to my clit, he probably ate me out for- i don't know how long but i came at least 3 times.

"azaire...please.." i whimpered trying to push his head away.

he leaned up and pulled his boxers down, his dick sprang out and has precum all over the head.

my eyes went to the veins on it as he took out a condom and slipped it on,"you comfortable like this?" he asked hovering over me.

"yes..."

he grabbed one of my legs putting it over his shoulder before slowly sliding in, my back arched off the seat as he stretched me open more and more.

"oh- azaireee." i whined as he stayed still and i could feel him throbbing inside me.

"goddamn...you so f-fuckin tight." he groaned before kissing me and started off with slow strokes

my hands immediately went to his back pulling him closer to me if possible, he leaned up looking down where we connected as he thrusted himself inside of me.

i watched as he took my other leg placing it on his shoulder as well, his hands planted on either side of me on the seat and he started going faster.

i moaned and cried as he started hitting me spot with no mercy or signs of slowing down, i watched as his chain moved with him and his teeth sank into his bottom lip.

"i love...yo ass so fuckin much.." he said before kissing me.

"i lov— fuck! i love you more!" i moaned feeling myself cum around him.

he let out a chuckle before pulling out and i noticed the condom was full, he took it off throwing it into a plastic bag before sitting up.

he pulled me into his lap holding me close and rubbing my back as my legs lightly shook. he peppered kisses all over my face and neck.

"you okay ma?" he asked me and i nodded pecking his lips.

he continued holding me and was just looking over my face,"bae you gotta hickey..." i mumbled poking the area.

"it'll be ight..." he said as i straddled his lap.

" what y- sh-shit..." he groaned as i slowly sunk down onto his length.

"baby...you g-gotta let up or imma nut in you." he warned holding my waist.

"azaire..." i moaned quietly feeling his dick twitch inside of me.

"man- fuck it..." he grumbled holding my waist and started thrusting into me from the bottom.

i wrapped my arms around his neck and he pulled me closer to him,"bounce..." he said into my ear while smacking my ass.

i don't know what had gotten into azaire but he was turning me every way but loose tonight.

# Chapter 20

♥

**X** ylah sailor summer

"sissy!!" kamari yelled running into the kitchen.

"wassup?" i asked as jamari followed behind him.

"can we have some?" kamari asked staring at the pancake mix.

"i don't care..why y'all still up?" i asked looking at the time on the oven seeing it was going on 1am.

"i don't know." jamari shrugged as he sat at the island.

i shook my head and focused on mixing while staring at my phone screen.

azaire: i love you baby, imma text you when i get done

-how long⬚

azaire: 2 hours max i promise, i'll call you when i get home

-okay i love you too, be safe

azaire loved 'okay i love you too, be safe'

azaire: always

-azaireeeee it's been 3 hours, you okay??-baeeeeee-baby⬚-what position y'all in-i'm playingggg...yo location not popping up delivered i wasn't trying to think he was cheating on me...there's no way he would.

i turned on the stovetop and put butter in a pan and waited for it to warm up, i sighed and grabbed my phone and to text the group chat.

-yallll

ayani: yes ma'am

sage: yoooo

-wyd

sage: waiting on taylin

ayani: watching baddies

-you stay watching ts

ayani: girlll ts be having me heated asf

sage: don't make sense y'all wanna go drunk bowling tmrw?

-yess sounds fun, except i'm not drinking too much

ayani: girl that damn hangover had yo ass

sage: LMAOOO but yes we can def do that

i put my phone down and started making pancakes for myself and the twins,"can we watch a movie in the living room?" jamari asked as i flipped the pancake.

"yeah what y'all wanna watch??" i asked.

"mm- cars?" kamari suggested.

"go pick which one." i said and they both took off to the living room making me laugh.

the back door opened and i jumped but calmed down seeing it was namari walking in with low red eyes.

"i don't know where yo boyfriend get his weed from...but that shit exotic." she said shaking her head and i laughed.

"imma tell him stop selling to you." i said and she waved me off.

"you needa tell him to not leave marks on you." she said pointing to her neck and i quickly covered my neck with my hand.

"umm namari you and mama have hickeys on y'all necks daily soo.." i trailed off.

"different- we grown." she said grabbing a pancake and walked out the kitchen.

i finished cooking and cleaned up my mess then gave the twins their plates before fixing my own and sitting in the living room with them.

they had already started the movie so i sat and watched with them while eating until i started getting sleepy. my stomach was starting to hurt from all the syrup.

i pulled my blanket over my body and laid down as the twins recited half the lines in the movie.

i groaned as i heard my phone ring, i lazily reached for it clicking accept,"m-ma..." i heard azaire's voice.

"baby?" i mumbled sitting up rubbing my face.

"i lo- fuck i love yo ass s-so fuckin much.." he said followed by a groan.

"are you okay?" i asked sitting up feeling my heart drop to my stomach.

"i- shit.."

"azaire!! nigga get the car!" i heard benz's voice.

"azaire what's going on??" i asked and i could hear coughing and yelling.

"xylah...i...i n-need you to s-say it back." he groaned.

"i love you more but baby-"

"b-benz i can't s-see ..." azaire mumbled.

i heard shuffling,"xylah! meet us at north hospital!" benz yelled into the phone before the call dropped.

i jumped from the couch running to my room, i quickly grabbed a hoodie and slippers.

i grabbed my car keys and left out the front door, my head was going everywhere thinking about everything that just happened in a matter of seconds.

i rushed into the hospital spotting the gang except benz and azaire already sitting there along with azaire's parents, honestly i was out of breath and my words felt stuck in my throat.

sage was the first one to spot me and she quickly walked towards me pulling me into a hug. i didn't hug her back i stood there and waited for someone to start talking.

"come wit us.." ayani mumbled and we all walked into the bathroom.

"xylah- i'm sorry...taylin told us a lil, they were making a deal and shit went left..azaire jumped in front of benz..azaire's currently in surgery so is benz.."

"benz ended up getting shot along with azaire.." ayani said and i slowly nodded letting the information sink in bedore i felt tears in my eyes.

"no don't cry- do you want a hug?" sage asked and i shook my head no wiping my eyes.

"come on we're gonna go back and wait..." ayani said and i followed them back to the waiting room.

i could feel everyone's eyes on me but i ignored their gazes by sitting down and staring at the floor infront of me, i crossed my arms holding them against my stomach.

"taylin...you need to calm down.." i heard sage say.

"yeah..get up real quick..." i glanced over at them and i saw sage get up and taylin stormed out the hospital.

"just let him breathe...he blames himself..." ayani said to sage who nodded.

"i know he does...that's why i'm scared for him to be by himself right now. when he's upset he self destructs." sage said with a sigh.

soon seconds turned into minutes into hours.

as time went on the feeling in my stomach wasn't getting better, my mouth was dry and my eyes kept watering.

i was so fuckin scared.

"family of blaine miller??" a nurse called out and i noticed two people stand up looking like they were related to benz.

definitely were.

we also paid attention as the nurse started talking,"alright...he's waking up out of surgery, he's going to need a lot of bed rest these next few weeks so make sure he takes it easy. you may go and see him if you would like to."

his im guessing parents nodded and quickly followed her,"go ahead..." sage whispered to ayani who shook her head.

"his parents don't know anything about me...i'll wait till they leave." ayani said.

"these two started meddling behind our backs..." sage explained noticing the confused look on my face.

i nodded and chewed on my lip,"you wanna go talk to a nurse with me?" marie asked me making me look at her.

i didn't want to talk but i got up following behind her.

"yes ma'am how may i help you?" a nurse asked looking up from her computer.

"i was wondering if they're any updates on azaire carmine..." she said and the nurse started typing.

"well...he just got out of surgery..umm i'll have a doctor come talk to you.." she trailed off before getting up.

"i'm sure- xylah honey you look like you're going to pass out. do you feel okay?" she asked and went to touch my forehead and i moved back.

not trying to be rude. i just didn't want to be touched.

i just shook my head and she frowned lightly,"ma'am is your husband here with you?" a doctor asked holding a clipboard.

"aaron." marie called and he quickly got up walking towards us.

"azaire..im sorry are you family?" the doctor asked staring at me.

nigga...

"she is. now please." aaron said sharply and the doctor cleared his throat looking down at the clipboard.

"he's alive and we removed the bullets..but he slipped into a coma." he said and his words started ringing in my ear as my vision blurred.

"will he wake up?" marie asked.

"that i can't tell...it's up to him but from a doctor's opinion-"

my eyes failed me and wouldn't stay open.

# Chapter 21

♥

"Princess...you have to eat.." namari told xylah.

xylah looked at the mcdonald's in namari's hand before shaking her head.

it's been two weeks since azaire's been in a coma, and everyday xylah had been there staying the night whenever she could.

her parents making sure to bring her a change of clothes along with her computer so she could still get school work done. but they noticed how her whole aura had changed dramatically since azaire been hospitalized.

not to mention xylah hasn't spoken a word since that night, she'd hold azaire's hand most the time not even touching her phone much.

she'd watched whatever random shows came on the tv in the hospital and fall asleep on the uncomfortable couch in the room but she didn't care. she wanted to stay by azaire's side by any means.

"xylah baby i love you but this isn't healthy you barely eat now.." matiyah said frowning noticing her daughter could go days without eating and still wouldn't say anything.

xylah sighed grabbing the mcdonald's bag from namari.

she looked inside seeing nuggest and fries with ranch.

xylah only took the fries, she placed two in her mouth and slowly chewed. once she swallowed her mouth started watering and she let out a small gag before putting the rest back.

"princess..." namari quickly said rubbing her back, xylah stared between her parents before bursting into tears.

namari quickly pulling xylah into a hug, xylah sobbed onto her hoodie.

matiyah's heart broke watching xylah finally break down, the whole two weeks she had been emotionless with everyone.

namari rubbed xylah's back as matiyah sat down beside them, xylah leaned up wiping her now puffy eyes.

they noticed azaire's machines started going off, he remained motionless but his heart rate was speeding up.

matiyah quickly went to grab a doctor while xylah stood up to grab his hand, right as she did his heart rate started going back down as the doctors walked in.

"we're just gonna check a few things." a doctor said and they carefully left the room being met with azaire's parents.

"what's going on?" marie quickly asked.

"his heart rate started going up...they're checking him now." matiyah said and marie nodded before holding out her had.

"i wish us meeting was under different circumstances, i'm marie this is my husband aaron." marie said and matiyah smiled shaking her hand.

"i'm matiyah and this is my wife namari, and of course you know our daughter xylah." matiyah said.

"yes she's a wonderful girl to our son." aaron said.

"and your son is just as good to her.." matiyah said.

meanwhile xylah had been zoned out and staring at the hospital floor counting the different squares to fight the urge of passing out.

"excuse us.." namari said noticing xylah looked slightly pale and pulled her to the bathroom.

"have you been sleeping?" namari asked xylah.

xylah nodded her head lying, she was sleeping on and off, waking up at every small noise she heard hoping either azaire was waking up or someone was texting her he had woken up.

it was a knock on the door waking xylah up, she looked over at the door as she turned on the hospital couch.

"wassup sis." benz said walking in followed by the rest of the gang.

xylah sat up on the couch so ayani and sage could sit down, "you've been okay?" ayani asked and xylah simply nodded.

it was weird silence until they started talking about random things they've all done and what not.

xylah was listening but she was also zoned out and was staring hard at azaire, she was hoping and praying he would start showing signs of waking up cause so far it was nun.

benz had been put on crutches due to his injuries and no matter what nobody could make him stay in one place, he always wanted to run with taylin so they could get revenge for the shit that happened.

"hmm.." sage said handing xylah a bottle of water.

she noticed xylah looked completely out of it, dried tears and bags under her eyes.

xylah gave her a small smile before opening the water and took small sips.

"he's gonna be ight xylah." taylin spoke and she nodded.

she was tired of hearing everyone say the same thing, she wanted him to get up and say himself he was fine.

the thought alone had her eyes watering and she sniffled before getting up and walking out the room.

she walked to the bathroom down the hall where she found herself sobbing in the stall, no matter how hard she tried to stop the tears they would keep coming.

she started feeling lightheaded from all the crying and tried to catch her breath before she felt her stomach turn and she was hunched over the toliet throwing up the few fries she ate along with bile.

her eyes watered from the burning in her throat and stomach, she went to the sink and splashed water on her face before using paper towels to clean her hands and face.

she walked out the bathroom and back to the room,"oh we was just finna leave- you ight?" benz asked xylah and she nodded walking back to her spot on the couch.

"if you need anything you know to text us boo." sage said.

soon enough they all left and xylah scooted a chair closer to azaire's bed and held his hand in hers.

she stared over his features, he still looked the same to her except you could tell his body was loosing a little weight along with muscles. when he was up and active he stayed in the gym and now he hasn't in two weeks due to his state.

she reached into her bag and pulled out a small container of vaseline and placed it on his lips before pecking his cheek.

she noticed his heart rate go up before quickly going back down after.

she smiled small while playing with his fingers.

# Chapter 22

♥

A zaire kade carmine

i felt stuck. everything felt stuck.

i could make out certain noises, some as people talking...machines going off. doors opening and closing.

along with what sounded like puking or coughing.

"mane....this wasn't supposed to be you, i was supposed to be the one hooked up to everything not you..why the fuck would you jump in front of me dawg...?" i heard followed by a sniffle.

i'm pretty sure it was benz speaking to me.

"shit xylah you scared the fuck outta me." i heard him say as a door opened.

i didn't her her voice though. i haven't heard it at all but other people have mentioned her name.

"...you've been doing okay? you drunk any water today?" i heard ayani's voice.

"sage and taylin bringing us some wendy's...i know you've been on they spicy nuggets bad lately." benz said.

then their words started sound disoriented.

i felt someone's hand in mine and i tried to think hard.

only xylah's hand is this soft.

i tried to squeeze her hand and i only felt my finger move.

"oh shit- you okay xylah?" i heard sage's voice.

"i..." i finally heard xylah's voice followed by a machine beeping rapidly.

"why his shit doing that?" i heard taylin before my eyes finally opened landing on all of them.

"oh shit— he's up! move!" benz yelled running out the room taylin right behind him.

it hit me...i'm in a hospital.

my eyes looked at all the girls, staying on xylah.

she had on my hoodie and my sweatpants, her hair was in a messy ponytail and a scarf around her head.

she was looking at me with wide eyes.

wait— i can't breathe.

i started moving around going for my mouth,"no! no azaire wait you can't the nurse has to get it!" ayani quickly said moving my hands down.

a few nurses and doctors walked in after making everyone get out the room.

my eyes felt heavy again and i was fighting the urge to close them all over again.

"yes i promise he is awake...he's probably gonna be very tired and weary at first but he's fine and should make full recovery.." i heard and felt someones hand in mine.

i opened my eyes groaning and trying to clear my throat, it felt sore as shit.

"oh my gosh azaire!" i heard my mom say before hugging me.

i hugged her back to my best ability since certain parts of my body was sore,"hey mama— where's.."

"she's in the bathroom son." my dad spoke up before i could finish.

"can you get her?" i asked my mama and my mama nodded walking out the room.

"what happened?" my dad asked once the door closed.

"not..not right now." i mumbled trying to sit up.

he helped me adjust the bed,"taylin and benz told me what they could...but i need to hear it from your point of view azaire." he said seriously and i nodded.

the door opened again and xylah walked in first then my mama, xylah walked towards the bed and gave me a small smile and i looked over her appearance.

she had bags under her puffy eyes, and her nose looked slightly swollen. maybe i'm tripping.

"damn i can't get a hug ma?" i asked and she broke down in tears before hugging me.

i pulled her onto the bed with me and i felt her tense up,"relax...i'm good.." i told her knowing she was probably trying to be careful of shit i was hooked up to.

i kissed her cheek as she laid her head on my chest and was hanging onto me tight,"we'll be right back.." my mama said and dragged my dad behind her.

"baby..." i said to her and she sat up to look at me.

"i...i missed you.." she said before holding her throat.

"you need my water?" i asked holding the cup towards her and she shook her head.

"i missed you too...i figured you was here...i always heard someone saying yo name." i said and watched her eyes lit up some.

"i stayed the night with you sometimes..." she said softly then made me drink some water from the cup the doctors gave me.

"did you talk to me?" i asked her and she frowned before shaking her head.

"i didn't talk to anyone..."

"so you've been quiet to everyone ma?" i asked and she nodded. "why?"

"i just couldn't talk...i was scared to lose you azaire." she said and her eyes watered again making me pull her back to my chest.

"i'm here ma..." i said pecking her lips.

"i was so fuckin scared azaire...the doctors said it was a slim chance of you waking up...and you were gonna leave us.." she said burying her face in the crook of my neck.

"im sorry baby.." i said kissing her cheek.

"the gang was here a lot too...along with our parents." she said and i nodded.

"i constantly was hearing the gang." i said making her laugh.

"so you know ayani and benz-"

"i was the one told him to go for it." i said and she nodded before sniffling.

"but now we gotta make sure you start sleeping baby. and you wearing my-" i stopped when i put my hand underneath the hoodie she was wearing.

she tensed up once my hand rubbed her stomach,"xylah..." i said lifting her hoodie up and saw her stomach had more of a pudge.

"hmm?" she mumbled looking everywhere but me.

"it's sumn you need to tell me?" i asked.

"you're gonna be a dad..." she mumbled as i grabbed her chin making her look at me.

"who else knows?" i asked.

"the nurse who made me realize.." she said.

"shit..." i groaned sitting my head back against the bed.

"are you mad? i'm—"

"chill out.." i said pecking her lips.

"i just ain't expect to wake up- how far are you?"

"5 weeks..." she said before adding,"you've been in a coma for 6..."

"what else have i missed?" i asked.

"that's it..." she said and i smiled before kissing her lips.

"we gonna be okay ma." i said and she smiled back before pulling the hoodie back down.

"once the nurse found out i was...she made sure i started eating because i wasn't at all..i had a eating problem but she made me realize it was another life inside me." she said and i nodded.

"well...i'm glad you having my first baby pretty, i promise imma be here for everything else." i said holding her.

"when do you wanna...tell everyone?"

"that's up to you..you the one that's gonna have to carry and start showing." i said and she nodded.

"it's still pretty early...so i think i wanna wait a lil longer."

i nodded,"you needa let everyone know you out of your mute shit." i said and she shook her head no.

i sighed and placed my hand under her hoodie to rub her stomach, i noticed her eyes starting to flutter.

"go to sleep imma be here when you wake up..." i told her kissing her forehead.

"i love you..." she said followed by a soft snore.

"i love you more baby.." i told her as a nurse walked into the room.

"i'm guessing she told you the news..."

"yes ma'am." i said and she nodded.

"imma tell you now azaire...you have a special girl, make sure you keep her close and give her everything she needs...especially now while she's carrying the baby. try not to have her stressing anymore."

# Chapter 23

♥

A zaire kade carmine

"azaire you need to relax.." mama said as i pulled my hoodie over my body.

"mama i have...i needa go check on xylah and i have therapy.." i mumbled.

"just invite her over-" i cut her off.

"mama i've been in the house for the past 3 weeks straight, i get food delivered here...the gang comes over here. i'll be fine." i said and she pouted as my dad walked in the room.

"marie the boy is fine-"

"you shut up talking to me." she pointed at him and dad sighed.

mama found out what all led to me being in the coma and she's been on both our asses ever since.

"marie come on." dad said pulling mama out my room and i sighed.

i checked my phone hearing it go off a few times.

xylah: how you feeling today?

-i'm doing better i didn't need to take any medicine today, what about you?

xylah: nauseous and lightheaded

-you've been drinking more water?

xylah:....nope

-xylah drink some fuckin water gang, you know that nurse gave you that bottle for a reason

xylah: but she wants me to drink like 4 of those in one day

-you need it for hydration ma

xylah: i guess..i'm coming over today?

-nah imma come see you

xylah: really? your mom letting you leave the house? you sure you don't need to stay home more

-it's been 3 weeks i'm good

xylah: okay i love you

-i love you more pretty

i put my phone in my jean pocket before grabbing my keys and walking out the house.

i checked my phone again once i got in the car seeing the boys text our group chat before they started a facetime call.

"yooo! azaire yo ass finally out the house." taylin said once the call connected.

"i thought ma dukes was gonna keep you there forever." benz said.

"she trying— she still pissed at us, mostly my dad." i said starting my car.

"damn...what you finna get into?"

"therapy and see xylah..." i said before we went off into a different topic.

i hung up once i got to my therapists building, i checked in before walking straight to her office.

"azaire it's been a minute..." she said and i nodded.

we had been having zoom meetings while i was in the house.

"well it's one thing i can say...your stutter has seemed to improve a lot since you've come out the coma..." she said and it hit me.

i haven't stutter since waking up...

"oh shit...oh shit you right." i said getting excited and she laughed.

"do you think it'll last?"

"i believe if it does come back it isn't gonna be as bad or frequent."

i watched xylah walk around her kitchen before laughing,"what's funny?" she asked mugging me.

"baby...you gonna have to tell them soon." i said and she frowned.

"huh?"

"baby you starting to walk differently." i said and she stopped moving completely.

"you serious?" she asked and i nodded.

"it's nothing crazy, it ain't a full pregnant waddle but- i can tell the difference and i'm sure if you're parents pay as much attention as i do..." i trailed off.

"well...it makes since why earlier namari was staring at me harder then usual but i just brushed it off." she said.

"how you think they gonna react?"

"i don't know...but i'm scared what if they get mad. or try to kick me out?" she asked and i noticed the tears in her eyes.

"ma...it's gonna be okay either way it go. now yeah they might get upset cause at the end of the day we still young...we still living under their roofs. but i know for a fact if they don't have our back i got us, okay? i got enough in my savings for us to get our own apartment if needed." i said as she wiped her face.

i pulled her into my embrace as she quietly cried,"i know...i have money saved up too it's just..i wasn't trying to become a parent yet.

but i'm also not really upset cause it's with you..and i trust you're gonna be there." she said and i nodded.

"i get what you saying...we gonna be ight ma." i said kissing her forehead.

"bae...you haven't been stuttering." she said and i smiled.

"i know.." i said and pecked her lips.

she had on one of my hoodies and tights so you couldn't really see her pudge unless you lifted the hoodie.

she backed up from me as the front door opened, her mom and namari walking in the kitchen.

"ugh this negro back?" namari asked and matiyah smacked her upside the head.

"stop, hey azaire how you been boo?" matiyah asked giving me a side hug.

"yeen gotta hug him." namari mumbled and matiyah waved her off.

"i've been okay ma'am, how about y'all?" i asked.

"good— i'd be better if you had you know..." namari mumbled.

"i can bring you back some later." i said shaking my head and namari handed me $30.

"get me what you can with that." she said grabbing matiyah's hand and lead her to the back door outside.

"azaire!" i heard the twins yell.

"wassup!" i laughed as jamari ran to hug me, kamari right behind him.

"are you staying the night?" kamari asked and i looked over at xylah who nodded her head.

"i can, just ask y'all parents." i said.

"they gonna say yes— come on! can you play 2k with us?" jamari asked.

"y'all get the game started and imma come in there." i told them and they ran towards the hall.

xylah was currently at air fryer fixing herself dino nuggets, i walked up behind her pressing her ass against me.

"bae..." she mumbled as i reached my hands underneath her hoodie to rub her stomach.

"lemme eat yo pussy..." i whispered in her ear and she shook her head.

"no yo tongue gonna poke it." she said and i busted out laughing.

"that's definitely not how it work ma." i said stepping back.

"you can, after you play wit my brothers." she said grabbing hot sauce from the cabinets.

"you gonna have my baby a damn hothead wit all that hot shit..." i mumbled and she rolled her eyes.

"do you know how you're gonna tell your parents?" xylah asked as i rubbed her feet.

"hell nah...my mama already still upset about be being so involved in the streets. but i'm really finna stop that shit now i gotta baby on the way. like....my dad was there but i wish he was there more and didn't have to leave at all times of night and shit, you know? i don't want my baby experiencing that." i said and she nodded with a small smile on her face.

"plus i can see how it affected you when...when i had to be in the hospital. ion want you to ever have to go through that again. imma have to just sit both my parents down and be straight up..." i said as she stared at me.

"i think imma wait until i can get an ultrasound and give them the picture. i'm just scared at the end of the day of their reaction." she said and i nodded.

"and i can understand....just know how ever shit end we gonna be good." i said and pecked her lips.

she moved to where she was straddling my lap and hugged me tightly, i wrapped my arms around her resting my hands on her ass.

"i love you..." she said softly.

"i love you more."

# Chapter 24

♥

**X** ylah sailor summer

"xylah...xylah.." i heard making me groan and slowly open my eyes.

"hmm?" i hummed pulling the cover over me.

"i done went to work and came back...and you're still asleep." mama said and i shrugged.

i was so fuckin tired.

i didn't want to get out from underneath my cover because i only had on boy shorts and a tank top, and my stomach definitely looked bigger without a hoodie.

"i stayed up last night..." i lied.

"xylah you needa go to sleep at night then...it's 4 o'clock." she said and my eyes widened

shit my appointment at 4:30!

"okayyy i'm finna get up...and go get sumn to eat." i said and she hummed.

"mhm...and when you get back i wanna talk to you." she said before i heard my bedroom door close.

my heart dropped to my ass as i peaked from under my covers. does she know?

i went to the bathroom and took a quick shower before calling the doctors office to let them know i'd be a few minutes late.

azaire: ma ain't no way you still asleepazaire:baby?azaire: xylah you better not miss this appointment azaire: i'm otw to get youazaire: you better be ready when i get there

azaire 6 missed calls

once i got done putting lotion on my body i slipped on my push up bra and underwear, i grabbed a pair of jeans to put on but stopped.

"wait..." i mumbled as i struggled to get them up over my thighs.

i felt my eyes water and shook my head,"this isn't the time.." i said more to myself as i started jumping to get them up.

it still didn't work...

that's when i broke down,"mama!" i yelled as tears poured down my face.

i heard her footsteps and the door opened,"what's wrong-" she stopped seeing my face then her eyes traveled down to my stomach.

"i'm sorry! i didn't mean to- and now my pants won't fit! please don't be mad at me!" i sobbed and she quickly pulled me into her arms as i cried.

"shhh....it's okay my love, look calm down the baby can feel everything you feel it's okay." she cooed.

"come on...i know you have some yoga pants..." she said and i nodded trying to stop crying.

"listen breathe...deep breaths xylah." she said.

she helped me change into stretchy pants then gave me a graphic t-shirt that was in my closet.

"you want me to put your socks on for you?" she asked and i shook my head no.

i put on my socks then slipped my black crocs on,"come here..." she said pulling me into her arms again.

"i'm not mad at you....do i wish you would have waited a lil longer? definitely but we can't go back in time. im gonna be here for you every step of the way, you're still young so i know it's nerve wrecking. i had you when i was 17 xylah...if you need anything you know you can ask me, okay? i love you so much." she said before kissing the side of my head.

i nodded wiping my face before she let me go,"can you not...tell the family yet, please?"

"of course we can keep this on the low for long as you want, it's your pregnancy nobody else's...now namari?"

"i'll tell her when i come back...she has a show tonight doesn't she?" i asked and she nodded.

"yeah by time you get back she should be here...azaire's car is outside." she said.

"okay...and thank you." i said feeling my eyes water again.

"it's no problem...stop crying baby it's okay." she said wiping my face again.

i grabbed my phone and walked out the house to azaire's car,"why you crying?" he asked grabbing my chin and kissed my lips.

"my jeans wouldn't fit...and my mama knows now.." i said and his eyes widened.

"now if you look closely...you can see your baby, now he or she is still very small since your only 8 weeks right now...but everything seems to be going smoothly..." the nurse said as she moved the wand around on my stomach.

i looked over at azaire and he's eyes looked glossy while he stared at the screen, he looked so focused and excited all at once.

"can we get pictures?" he asked, still hadn't looked away from the screen.

his hand gently squeezed mines as the nurse wiped the gel off my stomach,"of course...how many?" the nurse asked.

i watched as azaire started thinking,"about 4."

she left the room and azaire helped me sit up and fix my shirt,"i love you so much." he said then kissed my lips.

"i love you more..." i said kicking my legs.

"short ass.." he mumbled and i rolled my eyes.

"not too much...can we get wendy's spicy nuggets?" i asked.

"you gonna turn into a nugget, but yes ma. you want anything else?" he asked and i shook my head no.

"umm..i'm gonna tell namari when i get back home." i told him and he nodded.

"i might as well tell my parents this week too...just so everybody know." he said.

"when we gonna tell gang?" i asked and he shrugged.

"we still got that group chat wit all of them...just send yo ultrasound photo whenever you want." he said and i chewed on my lip.

"can you send it instead?" i asked and he laughed before nodding.

"i got you, i'll do it before this week over." he said.

"okay..." i said getting off the chair once the nurse walked back in with our photos.

"it look like a lil peanut or sumn..." i mumbled and azaire laughed shaking his head.

"alright your next appointment is gonna be next month but you can come earlier if you have any concerns." the nurse told us and i nodded.

"let's go i want a strawberry lemonade." i said grabbing azaire's hand and dragged him out the room.

we made it to his car and i reclined the seat feeling myself getting sleepy, i pulled out my phone and looked at my face.

it was definitely starting to get a lil fatter...and my nose looked different.

"baeee my nose." i complained as he pulled out the parking lot.

"what about it?" he asked glancing at me.

"it's like...i don't know bigger or swollen a lil." i pouted.

he stopped at a stop sign then leaned over to kiss my nose and lips,"you still look pretty ma." he said before pressing the gas.

i smiled then took a photo of the ultrasound on my phone then handed two of the pictures to him.

i was back home and azaire was back at his parents house, my stomach was now full but i was still hungry.

i didn't wanna bother him though when i knew he was still stressing about telling his parents.

i sat on the back patio and waited for namari to come out, the back door opened and i felt my heart beating faster.

"you needed me?" she asked sitting down in a chair beside me.

i had a blanket wrapped around me so she couldn't see my stomach.

i nodded my head,"so..." i started as she started rolling up.

"pothead..." i mumbled and she stopped rolling to look at me.

"xylah..." she said and i groaned before throwing the ultrasound picture in her lap.

she froze.

i froze.

maybe 30 seconds went by and she was still just staring at the picture.

"namari..." i said quietly.

i got up getting ready to walk inside,"aht aht sit down." she quickly said.

"you're not saying anything!" i whined.

"cause girl i'm tryna make sure i'm not dreaming....azaire know?" she asked and i nodded.

"i found out while he was in a coma..." i said and her eyes widened.

"you knew for that long?"

"namari-"

"look listen...i'm not gonna sit here and yell at you and what not. that shit pointless..but i do trust azaire as your boyfriend. y'all still young as hell but i can tell y'all love each other. it's just a huge ass responsibility. but you know i've always been here for you and imma continue to do that." she said and i felt the tears on my face.

"xylah don't cry princess it's okay. me and yo mama gonna be here for you no matter what happens, and you know this." she said standing up.

she pulled me into a hug and i started crying all over again,"calm down before you upset my grandchild." she said and i laughed.

"just don't get mad when he or she replace you as my favorite." she said and i smacked my lips.

"but next time i see azaire i'm putting belt to ass." she said shaking her head.

"now go inside while i smoke, my grandchild don't needa smell nun of this." she said.

i walked inside and sighed.

"what's that?" kamari asked pointing to the pictures in my hand.

"i gotta tell y'all sumn...but y'all can't tell anyoneee outside of these walls..okay?" i said sitting at the island with them.

"the fuck is that..." jamari mumbled pointing at the baby.

"first off that mouth...second y'all gonna be uncles." i said and kamari quickly snatched the photo up.

"you're pregnant?" jamari asked and i nodded.

"ewww you be having sex sissy?" kamari asked and i smacked my lips taking the photo back before he snatched it back.

"bye-"

"waittt! is it a boy or girl?" kamari asked and i shrugged.

"ion know yet." i said.

"i hope it's a boy." kamari said and they both continued looking at the photos making me smile.

# Chapter 25

♥

Few weeks later
    xylah sailor summer

"girllll yo stomach then swoleeee up." ayani said reaching over to rub my stomach.

ayani, sage and i were just leaving the nail salon and now we're going out to eat.

"i know..." i grumbled trying to get comfortable in the passenger seat.

"you wanna get some starbucks?" sage asked and i immediately perked up.

"please! i haven't had any in sooo long." i said adjusting my earbuds.

i had went sometime without wearing em but i was starting to get overstimulated easily lately so it was back to wearing hem.

i placed in an order for all of us and paid as she drove to the nearest one, that's when i went to text azaire

-baby daddy!

azaire: don't be calling me that

-but that's what you are

azaire: i'm yo husband spwm

-i'm soooo sorry husband

azaire: you getting starbucks?

-i forgot yo card connected to my account

azaire: you never showed me your nails...lemme see the baby

i sighed as i took my phone and adjusted my phone to snap a clear photo of my stomach.

azaire loved an image

azaire: how you feeling tho? you've been dizzy lately?

-no i'm just extra hungry and my feet hurt a lil

azaire: when y'all get back to the apartments i'll rub yo feet

-thank youu ⌧

azaire: you gonna have to take your belly ring out sooner or later

-no imma get that maternity belly ring ion want my piercing to close⌧

azaire:mmm lmk what kind you want so i can order it

-babyyy i can get it myself

azaire: no

i shook my head as we pulled up into the starbucks drive thru,"i have a mobile order for xylah." ayani spoke then pulled around in line.

"y'all thought of any baby names yet?" sage asked and i shook my head no.

"no we're waiting until we found out the gender." i said playing with my belly ring.

"ohh, i'm team boy." sage said and ayani laughed.

"oh im team twins." ayani said then looked over at me.

"i'll die— no offense to my mama but ion see how she did it...plus the twins heads big as hell." i said and they laughed.

"girl why you bullying your brothers?" sage asked and i shrugged.

"alright keep talking shit, that baby gonna come out looking like a lollipop." ayani said and i huffed.

"no it won't- stop speaking on my child." i said as we pulled up to the window.

i pulled a few dollars out my phone case for tips then quickly grabbed my drink, i took a few sips of the frape and felt the urge to pee already.

"i ain't even drunk nun foreal..." i mumbled adjusting myself in the seat.

"can you please pull to the front?" i asked ayani.

"you gotta tinkle?" sage asked and i waved her off as ayani did what i requested.

"fuck my babydad bow bow bow bow bow- this that bootymeat!" i sung as i walked past the boys who were high off they asses.

"xylah." azaire said following right behind me.

"i gotta peee." i laughed as he grabbed my waist and pecked my lips.

"mhmm...stop singing that shit." he said following me into the bathroom.

clingy?

i always follow my bf to the bathroom whenever i'm wit him at first he looked at me weird but now he just use to it.

i sat on the toliet while he looked at himself in the mirror running his hand over his waves,"i needa haircut..." he mumbled.

"no cause you just tryna look good for no reason." i said mugging him.

"bae..." he said looking over at me and i rolled my eyes getting up to wipe then washed my hands.

"yes?" i said looking up at him once he stood in front of me.

he grabbed my waist pulling me closer to him then leaned down to kiss me, i kissed him back slipping my hands into his sweats.

"get yo freak ass on." he laughed pulling away from me and i pouted.

"baeee." i whined.

"baby our friends not far at all— look i gotchu later." he said and i rolled my eyes walking past him back to the living room.

"who made you mad?" benz asked looking at me while he rubbed ayani's legs.

"yo fuck ass homeboy." i mumbled then felt a pop on my thigh as azaire sat beside me.

"don't start..." he said pulling my feet on his lap and started taking off my forces.

i sighed as he rubbed my feet, it felt good as fuck.

"you needa start wearing slides more so your feet can relax, they starting to swell a lil." he said and i nodded.

"you never told me how your parents reacted.." i said and he sighed still rubbing my feet.

"my mama ain't talking to me...my dad said he's gonna be there and he just warned me about the sleepless nights and what not. he also said if i really want a apartment he'll help me get one." he said and i smiled for the dad part but-

"why yo mama not talking to you?" i asked and he shrugged.

"ion know...she just looked at me like she was really disappointed then she got up and left the room, she still won't talk to me now no goodmorning or nothing. " he said and i could tell it affected him.

"im sure she'll come around....cause how much you wanna bet when the baby get here oh she gonna wanna be all over em." i said and he shrugged.

"it's whatever, i still got my dad on my side so. plus im pretty sure she still upset with the street shit..." he said before pulling me into his lap.

i sat with my back against his chest and his hands rested on my baby bump.

"gang what you gonna do for yo birthday?" taylin asked.

"ion know yet...ion wanna do much foreal." azaire said.

"plus xylah pregnant i ain't tryna do a lot." he added.

"don't use me as an excuse, you turning 18 you needa go out bae. i'll be okay." i said moving around to sit comfortably.

"i don't wanna do nun if you ain't gonna be there." he said rubbing my thighs.

"i'll be there, just don't have me standing for a long time and make sure a bathroom there- actually let me plan your birthday." i said.

"yeah that's not happening." he said and i pouted.

"don't be lame, let's see what she can come up wit." benz said.

"that part, and if she need help she can ask one of us." ayani said.

"pleaseee bae i promise it'll be worth it." i said and he groaned.

"fine but don't spend alot of money xylah i'm not playing." he said and i nodded.

"i won't- you want some strippers?" i asked turning in his lap and he popped my lip.

"don't let no stupid shit fall from yo mouth." he said making me pout and hold my lip.

"yo daddy just popped me...we gonna jump him when you come." i told my stomach and he laughed rubbing my stomach.

"yeah we'll see." he said kissing my cheek then lip.

# Chapter 26

♥

## Azaire kade carmine

"babyyy....azaire get uppp." xylah dragged shaking my body. i groaned as i turned over in her bed,"wassup??" i grumbled.

"come on...we gotta doctor's appointment." she said and i slowly sat up seeing i was still dressed.

walmart vest and all.

i came to her house after getting off work and immediately crashed as soon as she made me lay down. i wouldn't deny i had been tired taking shifts left and right.

"you need to stop working overtime so much, we're gonna be fine baby." she said before kissing all on my face.

"i know...but i just wanna make sure.." i mumbled walking to her bathroom to brush my teeth.

i brushed my teeth and washed my face then xylah came in with clothes,"you leave your clothes over here sometimes soo...i washed these jeans and shirt for you along with boxers." she said sitting them on the sink.

"thank you baby." i said kissing her forehead then her nose and lips.

i looked at her outfit, black leggings with a black cropped tank top and jean jacket on top.

"you look good..." i said kissing her lips.

"thank you- now take your shower." she said walking out the bathroom.

"azaire.." xylah said knocking me out my trance.

"you still thinking about it?" she asked and i smiled harder if possible.

"i'm just happy as fuck we having a boy ma, you?" i asked as i cut up my pancakes.

"i'm excited, i hope he's a mamas boy." she said and i shrugged.

"no telling, i mean i like being under you so he probably will too." i said and she took a bite from her hashbrown.

once she finished she spoke,"so imma have two clingy people on me, that's crazyyy." she said and i laughed.

"i gotta ask you sumn?" i asked her and she gave me her full attention.

"when we first met...and you said you wanted to be a stay at home mom..do you still want to?" i asked her and she shrugged.

"i mean....yeah but ion think it's possible right now." she said.

"what if it is tho?" i asked and she raised her eyebrows.

"but we both still live with our parents...plus i'm still in schoolll." she said and i nodded.

"i'm not saying you have to decide right now...hell we can even wait until after our son gets here. i do want us staying under the same roof sooner or later just so it'll be easier for us with him and we'll have our own space." i said and she pursed her lips together.

"i get what you're saying...and i do online school so you know that isn't really much of a problem. we both have our own cars. what about you tho?" she asked.

"right now walmart is just so i can keep making money, cause i'm not fully out the streets but i'm working my way out. my dad already has me doing this program so i can start becoming a web developer...and based on the program it won't take too long for me to really start making money from it." i said and she nodded.

"i mean...we can think on it some more and in a few months i'll really let you know what i think." she said making me smile.

"okay, i'm good with that...you got anything together yet for my birthday?" i asked and she nodded.

"yes i do, and i'm not telling you nun." she smiled before taking a sip of her orange juice.

"fair i guess...what you doing today?" i asked her and she shrugged.

"i might go wit my mama to her store and get a few hours there in...you?" she asked.

"i work tonight." i said and she sighed.

"you should call out and come wit me to namari's gallery tonight." she said.

"it's too late for me to call out." i said and she groaned.

"tell them your girlfriend pregnant and sick." she said.

"ma-"

"pleaseeeee." she begged.

"this the only time, no more after this." i said pulling my phone out.

"okay, thank youuuu." she said getting up and came to my side to hug me and kissed my cheek.

i pulled into my driveway and sighed seeing the lights were still on so of course both of them were up.

i walked out to the front door and was about to unlock it until i heard yelling.

"just talk to me! you're acting childish wit this dumbass silent treatment- and not just to me but your own son!" my dad yelled.

"i wouldn't have to if you would've just listened to me in the first place! if you had just left the streets he probably would've never had the idea to even join!"

i carefully unlocked the door realizing they weren't in the living room but the kitchen, so i kept my footsteps quiet just to hear the rest.

"marie- you knew what kinda life i lived when you met me...i told you from the jump what it was and how i planned staying in this for a while. you told me you didn't care, you chose to stay.

and i can understand you're upset i let my son follow my footsteps but at least he doesn't want to forever. but you shouldn't be treating him the way you do when you stayed wit me while i lived the same life."

"aaron you should've never let him get involved in the same shit you were in. you know how the streets are— for godsake he woke up from a coma a few months ago...and now he's about to be a dad? how does that make you feel as a parent?" she asked.

"honestly....i'm proud of my son, cause even while he was in the streets he made sure to graduate from highschool. he could've decided to leave xylah once he found out she was pregnant but he didn't he goes to all of her appointments and he's deciding to leave the streets alone now.

you would know if you fuckin talked to him. yeah he could've waited a few years before bringing a baby in the world but he didn't. at least he's gonna be there for the baby.." he said shaking his head then his eyes landed on me before widening.

mama followed his gaze her eyes doing the same, i cleared my throat before speaking.

"the baby is a boy..." i simply said before walking to my room shutting and locking the door behind me.

i sighed sitting down on my bed and undressed leaving myself in my boxers.

i sighed as i started thinking back to everything they just said. i understand the streets isn't always the way to go...but it was never my main focus either.

i stayed on top of my school work and even played basketball, but i wasn't interested in college. i never planned to be bringing a baby into the world either but now i am. i wouldn't have it any other way honestly.

i'm just glad i'm having a baby with someone like xylah, she's honestly the most genuine and sweetest person i've ever met. she's went out her way with introducing me to everyone and even now hangs out with my friends.

she doesn't care about the lifestyle i have or the amount of money i can give her.

she's always loved me for me

i went to my phone and clicked facetime then found her name, it was really the main name on there.

"heyyyyy- what's wrong?" she asked as his face appeared in the camera.

"why sumn gotta be wrong?" i asked and she put her eye in the camera before backing up.

"cause the way your eyes look, and your mug is a lil deeper then usual. so what's wrong?" she asked and i sighed.

"i walked in while my parents were arguing...basically just talking about me i guess." i mumbled and she nodded.

i broke down small parts of what was said and she had the phone sitting up while she did her skin care.

"honestly i believe your mom just feels some kinda way because you did end up in the streets and of course you got hurt, but that's kinda apart of being in the streets. i'm not gonna say she should be surprised tho cause like you said your dad is also in the streets...y'all did shit together.

and i mean i would be surprised if my son came to me at 17 and was like he's gonna be a dad but at the end of the day everyone is human and does things. i would still love and support him though." she said after wiping her face with a towel.

"yeah..ion know i guess it's just her body language when she was talking about it. it's like she disgusted wit me or sumn xylah." i explained and got that weird feeling in my throat.

"i don't think she's— bae you finna cry?" she asked and i groaned.

"chill.." i mumbled honestly not wanting to.

"baby, it's okay. if you need to cry let it out...you can come back over if you want."

"nah imma be ight..." i said then went into my nightstand and pulled out my rolling tray along with backwoods.

smoke these feelings away.

# Chapter 27

♥

A zaire kade carmine

i watched xylah as she ate her spicy nuggets from wendy's, that's all she's been eating. anything spicy she had to have it or it was waterworks.

"i don't see how yo asshole don't be burning..." i mumbled and she looked at me.

"you said sumn?" she asked and i shook my head no.

"oh okay...cause i was finna say.." she said dipping her nuggets in ghost pepper ranch.

"hmm..." she mumbled holding it towards my mouth and i took a bite.

"you haven't been eating bae..." she said frowning.

"i do just not as much i ain't been hungry.." i said and i watched as she studied my face more.

"you high? when did you smoke?" she asked and i shook my head.

"i didn't smoke." i said.

"i took a perc when i was wit the boys earlier." i said.

"you usually take them?" she asked as she stuffed fries in her mouth.

"nah just wanted to see how they make me feel, feel stuck as shit..." i said rubbing my eyes.

"oh...how's things been at home?" she asked and i sighed.

"ion really wanna talk about allat..." i said placing my hand on her stomach.

i found myself smiling at the thought i was really finna have a whole ass son out here.

"baby..." she said knocking me out my trance.

"what's been going on?"

"mane...my mama still acting weird towards me, and it's like her and my dad arguing more. that shit aggravating to hear." i said and she grabbed my other hand and started playing with my fingers.

her ass love doing that shit.

"i'm sorry, you know you can always come over here." she said and i nodded.

"i know ma." i said kissing her forehead.

she finished her meal still feeding me fries and nuggets here and there, she drunk half her dr pepper then made me drink the rest.

"i'm still hungry." she frowned and i laughed.

"what else you want?" i asked and she shrugged.

"yo son said sumn spicy." she said and i laughed.

"he ain't say nun like that." i said as she sat on my lap.

"he said hot wings, with crinkled fries and a lotttt of extra ranch." she said and i shook my head grabbing my keys.

"come on so we can go get it." i said getting up and held her as i did so.

"i'm not heavy?" she asked and i held her up by her butt.

"never that, you still feel light ma." i said pecking her lips.

"stop imma get horny." she pouted and i laughed.

my phone started ringing back to back and i groaned reaching over to find it,"hel—"

"azaire where you at?" my mama asked in a sharp tone.

"i'm at xylah's-"

"you wit that fast lil girl?" she asked and my face immediately scrunched up.

"how the fu- bye bruh." i said hanging up.

she was finna get cussed out.

i felt xylah move around,"ma...i'm finna go home." i said and she whined.

"imma come back in the morning baby and we can go get sumn to eat, i promise." i said kissing her lips.

"okay...call me when you home please, i love you." she said kissing me back.

"i love you more ma." i said then put on my shoes and grabbed my keys.

i walked out their house making sure to lock the door then got in my car, i let the car warm up before connecting my phone to the aux and pulling out their driveway.

after driving a while my house came into view and i felt my mood dropping already.

i got out my car and walked inside after unlocking the door, my dad was in the living room watching tv and his eyes set on me.

"i thought you was staying wit xylah." he said and i shrugged.

"mama called asking where i was at..." i said and he rolled his eyes.

"yo mama been tripping..." he said as he turned up the volume on the tv.

"i'm what aaron?" mama asked as she walked down the hall.

"gone marie." he grumbled and mama made eye contact with me before waving her hand for me to follow her.

i followed her to the kitchen and she sat on one side of the island and i did sit on the other side.

i was waiting for her to say anything but she was just quiet and staring at me.

"so...you think you're ready to be a dad?" she asked.

"i mean....the baby is on the way, and i'm willing to do whatever to make sure he straight.." i said and she nodded.

"you sure the baby is yours?" she asked and a mug instantly came across my face.

"of course i do, why wouldn't i?"

"lemme guess you've been spending all kinda money on this one too? and now she's pregnant with your baby? azaire—"

"mama real shit shut up talking that bullshit, you ain't talked to me in weeks and this the first thing you wanna let come out my mouth?? talking about my girlfriend and she ain't even here to defend herself. plus you doing it while she carrying yo grandson. of course that's my fuckin baby all me and xylah do is be under each other unless we working or wit friends." i vented and she nodded.

"at the end of the day azaire, im still your mother so watch your mouth. im just saying the last few girls did some dirt and-"

"xylah's not them. and i can say with confidence she ain't never did me dirty." i said.

"i say you still need to get a dna test azaire...i just don't approve of you suddenly becoming a dad this fast." she said and i smacked my lips getting up.

"you should've stayed not talking to me bro." i said and i heard her get up as well.

"azaire don't walk away from me while i'm talking to you."

"mama ain't nun else to talk about, xylah having my baby and i'm not getting no dumb ass dna test when i know for a damn fact it's mines! i can understand you being upset or disappointed with me for having a kid early i get that!

but giving me the silent treatment and acting as if you disgusted with me is way different, then you sit there and try to talk about xylah? nah ion wanna hear that." i said then finally walked into my room slamming the door.

i sat down on my bed as my leg shook while i reached for my rolling tray. i groaned seeing all my weed was gone.

"mane fuck..." i grumbled feeling tears prick at my eyes.

the baby shower was this weekend, and i know my dad will most likely show up but my mama? i didn't even want her to come anymore.

especially if she was gonna have that weird ass energy.

i grabbed my phone and called xylah,"hello-"

"baby can i please come back over bro?" i asked and heard shuffling.

"yeah i can tell my brothers to unlock the door bae, you okay?"

"i will be once i'm back around you, imma take a shower then i'll be on the way."

"okay i love you, and take a few deep breaths bae yo nose red." she said.

"i love you more, i got you." i said before we hung up.

# Chapter 28

♥

Xylah sailor summer

"ouuu you look so pretty." sage said and i smiled as i looked in the mirror at myself.

"thank you, y'all look good too." i said looking over their outfits.

"mhm girl today about you and the babyyy." ayani said as she slipped on my heels.

"your slides already in the car cause i know you not gonna wear them the whole time..." azaire spoke up making me look his way.

we were all currently at taylin and sages apartment getting ready for my baby shower.

"okay thank you baby."

"you're welcome ma..imma be right back." he said kissing my cheek then walked out the room.

i put some final touches on my makeup then took the rollers out my hair, i had a black wig that was 20 inches, middle part with soft baby hairs.

i combed my hair to loosen some of the curls to my liking,"i think that's everything..." i said getting up and pulling my dress down.

my dress was a blue to match the theme of the cookie monster, it came all the way down to my ankles slightly dragging on the floor and was off the shoulders but clung to my body.

"okay so you ready for everything?" sage asked and i nodded grabbing my phone and purse.

"earbuds?" ayani asked and i pointed to my ears.

"already in." i said.

"aweee everything is so nice in here.." i said taking in the decorations while holding azaire's hand.

"yeah...yo family really did they shit." azaire said and i looked up at him to take in his appearance.

he had a fresh cut and was wearing a blue collared shirt with khaki pants and black forces.

no burberry? thank god.

a few chains around his neck and gold studs in his ears,"what's wrong?" he asked looking down at me and i shook my head.

"nothing...you just look really good." i said and he laughed pecking my lips.

"that's how she in this situation now, move." my granny said coming to hug me and i laughed hugging her back.

"aspen leave them alone, wassup azaire." grandma said to him.

"cant believe you making me a great grandma already..." grandma said shaking her head.

"i meannn at least y'all can still move around and stuff." i said and they both tilted their heads to the side.

"i ain't watching nun." granny quickly said crossing her arms.

"watch her be the first one tryna see the baby." grandma said putting her arm around granny.

granny rolled her eyes,"shut up tahani." she mumbled and i laughed.

"come on, let's go sit down and i'll make your plate." azaire said grabbing my hand and dragged me towards the table that was for us.

"azaire!" he turned around seeing his dad and i watched a smile stretch across his face.

"wassup." azaire said and gave him a quick hug.

"mama?" azaire asked quietly and aaron shook his head.

"oh...okay- it's fine at least everybody else here." azaire said and i noticed other family members of his were here except his mama.

time went on and everyone ate, played games, and we opened a few presents since it was so many the rest would just have to go back home with one of us.

"that's yo 5th cake pop xylah..." azaire said grabbing my waist and pulling me to him.

"i knowww but they so good..bite." i said holding it towards his mouth and he bit the rest of it off.

"a-zaire..." my voice cracked and i watched his eyes widened.

"my bad ma, it was only so much left- don't cry i can get you another." he said quickly wiping my tears.

"please..." i mumbled and he nodded walking towards the dessert table.

i sat down and carefully wiped my face remembering i had on makeup,"you enjoying everything so far?" i heard namari say as she took a seat beside me.

"yeah, thank y'all for doing all this...and being there for me. like i've heard other people's story about being pregnant young....and i'm really lucky to have family like y'all." i said and she nodded.

"you don't gotta thank me or us for being good people xylah. yeah not everybody gets that but you know how our family is. we don't play about each other. and we never play about our kids. i remember when i first met yo ass...you had me up playing wit you while yo mama was sleep." she said before laughing.

"i was asking yo non talking ass if it was fine if i fucked wit yo mama."

"not too much on me." i said laughing with her.

"have y'all thought of a name yet??" she asked and i nodded.

"i guess you can be the first to know...it's azriel sawyer carmine." i said.

"azaire and azriel...y'all wanna be like me so bad." she said and i smacked my lips.

"just cause you and the twins name rhyme don't mean we copying you." i said laughing.

azaire came back with my cake pop and i immediately took it starting to eat it,"i'm surprised you haven't dipped nun in hot sauce." namari said.

"oh nah her meatballs, mac and cheese, and chicken was all covered in it earlier." azaire said and i mugged him.

"she didn't need to know allat." i said and azaire took a sit back beside me placing his hand on my thigh.

namari left to go find my mama before aaron walked back over to us,"listen i'm finna go...but i needa give y'all sumn." he said making me pay attention to him.

he placed two keys in front of us, azaire and i looked at each other then back at aaron.

"umm dad what they for?" azaire asked.

"y'all house."

my heart dropped and i suddenly felt the urge to pee real bad. this baby stay on my damn bladder.

"i'm sorry...our who?" i asked.

"i already talked to your parents xylah...they agreed on y'all living under the same roof and it's not far from them."

"dad you bought us a house? we talked about renting apartments not-"

"i know what we've talked about and i trust you son, you've made me proud. i wanted to do this for you, xylah, and my grandson on the way...the house has 3 bedrooms and 2 bathrooms...y'all can decorate how y'all see fit." he said and i felt my eyes water.

"i...dad i can't take this. you didn't even let me pitch in on paying anything."

"use your money for the baby and furniture." aaron said sincerely.

"son...your mother and i are getting a divorce so the current house we're in is gonna get sold next year..." he said and i noticed azaire's mood droop some.

"a divorce? she's really that mad at me-"

"it has nothing to do with you. we haven't been seeing eye to eye lately and other things have happened with you not around...and i'm sure you wouldn't want to live with one of us now you're getting older." he said and azaire sighed.

"yeah...thank you, for everything." azaire said getting up and they embraced each other in a tight hug i could tell they both needed.

"shit...just remember everything i've taught you azaire, i expect nothing but the best from you, you hear me?" aaron said once pulling back from the hug and blinked his eyes rapidly.

"yeah i hear you, i promise i won't let you down." he said and aaron said his goodbyes to me before leaving.

"i can't believe this..." azaire mumbled looking down at the keys.

"me either..." i mumbled,"i'm sorry about you know..your—"

"ion wanna talk about her right now ma...but can i later tonight?" he asked and i immediately nodded.

"yeah of course..." i said kissing his lips and he smiled at me before pulling me into his lap.

his face instantly going to the crook of my neck,"i love you so much..." he mumbled and i heard a sniffle.

"bae you gonna make me cry.." i pouted and he laughed quietly.

"i'm not trying to, you just do so much for me without even knowing xylah." he said rubbing my waist.

# Chapter 29

♥

Few weeks later

xylah sailor summer

i groaned as i sat down on the bed in the airbnb,"can you get off my bladder so i can finish this room for yo daddy?" i mumbled to my stomach while pressing on it.

i felt a kick in response and found myself smiling,"you would move while he not here...you better do it again later too.." i said before getting up and looked over the room.

"yeahh i did good." i said more to myself as i looked over how everything came out.

i just decorated the room we were sharing, everything else was regular besides the kitchen having different foods and alcohol for them.

"xylah! they pulling up in the driveway!" ayani yelled and sage ran into the room.

"you need- DAMNNN girl he better dick you down this is niceee." she said making me laugh.

i had on a brown dress that had spaghetti straps and hugged my body and came all the way down to my ankles with gucci slides.

"thank you." i said before we both walked back to the living room.

i tried not to laugh as benz and taylin lead a blindfolded azaire into the house.

"on my son if y'all tryna see me up i'm haunting the fuck out y'all asses." he spat wit a mug on his face.

"you aggressive as fuck for nun." benz mumbled and i grabbed one of azaire's hands watching his face soften.

"ma?? y'all bought me to my baby?" he asked trying to move his blindfold.

"noo wait keep it on." i said and he smiled pulling me into a hug.

"this must be for my birthday?" he asked.

"yesss happy birthday bae again, now carefully walk." i said leading him to our bedroom while everyone stayed in the living room.

"okay take it off.." i said stepping back and he slowly undid it and i watched his eyes light up at the room.

then his eyes landed on me and he quickly picked me up spinning us around while i laughed hanging onto him.

it surprised me even tho the baby was making me gain weight azaire could effortlessly pick me up whenever he wanted.

"this shit— thank you so fuckin much ma." he said sitting on the bed with me in his lap.

"you're welcome...you like it right?" i asked and he licked his lips before speaking.

"i love this shit...and you paid for my haircut? yeah i promise imma wife yo ass once you 18." he said and i laughed.

"okay baby." i said standing up off his lap and looked over his outfit.

black nike tech with matching sweats and white air forces for once. he had on a few chains and silver earrings in his ears.

"you so fine stink." i said grabbing his face and kissed his lips.

he stood up keeping our lips connected and laid me on the bed moving stuff out the way,"wait, your presents..." i moaned as he kissed down my neck.

"i'll worry about them later." he said before pushing my dress up then my underwear to the side and slid two fingers inside me.

he sucked on my neck as he moved his fingers slowly while pulling my dress up more, he went back between my legs attached his mouth to my clit making my mouth go slack and my back arched off the bed.

"mmm...fuck bae." i moaned quietly as he gripped my thighs keeping me in place while tongue fuckin me faster.

he harshly sucked on my clit and almost immediately i started cumming while he continued eating me out,"f-fuck.." i whimpered as my legs shook.

"y'all i don't know..." i mumbled looking in the mirror at the outfit i wore.

"girl you look cuteee- i promise azaire ain't gonna be able to keep his hands off you." sage said and i messed with the skirt.

my stomach was definitely out, i hadn't wore sumn this revealing while being pregnant.

the skirt came mid-thigh and the top was cropped and tied in the front, so cleavage was definitely out as well. both pieces of clothing were a dark red.

we were currently in the club's bathroom, they ended up kinda sneaking me in because i wasn't 18 yet so.

"plus pregnant girls can have fun too, and you know azaire don't want you in here the whole time." ayani said as she fluffed out the curls in my wig.

"okay...let's go i guess." i mumbled and we all walked side by side to the section that was for azaire.

"ma! i missed youuu!!" he dragged once he seen me and held his arms out for me.

i laughed sitting on his lap and he quickly wrapped his arms around my waist and laid his head on my chest.

"i missed you more..how much has he had?" i asked benz who was definitely drunk as fuck.

"umm...damn what all you had gang?" benz asked and they both busted out laughing.

"i ain't gonna hold you i don't know." azaire said before looking up at me.

"you so sexy...i wanna give you another baby after this one..." he said and i shook my head.

"one is enough." i said running my hand over his waves.

"no it's not, you gotta give me a girl too ma...i wanna eat yo—" i placed my hand over his mouth.

"we infront of yo friends." i said.

"he said worse when you was gone.." taylin said shaking his head.

"bae me and benz shared a edible, i'm high as fuck but you look delicious." he said.

"thank you baby..." i said pecking his lips but he quickly grabbed my neck deepening the kiss.

"aht aht! don't fuck out hereee!" ayani said and i looked over seeing her cover her eyes.

"righttt." sage laughed before opening a bottle of luna and started pouring shots for everyone.

except me.

"hmm baby." i said handing azaire his shots.

he smiled and happily took it while the boys cheered him on,"can i get another kiss?" azaire asked with a pout.

"let the liquor settle down first.." i said then quickly grabbed the chili cheese fries i ordered.

"hmm..." i mumbled holding a fry to his mouth and he happily took it.

he rubbed my stomach while i ate, he was also rapping almost every song that came on.

i finished eating and wiped my hands off as a song came on instantly making azaire tap my leg.

i got up and he grabbed my hand pulling me down to the floor with him and everyone else.

Late nights, I reminisce about you, it's hard to forget about youI swear I can't live with you, but I can't live without youJump off a plane on an island, and I'm here without youAin't left my hotel in three days, I feel sick without you, sick without you

"my stomach do this turninggg i feel sick without ya." azaire sung to me while holding my waist.

"my closest friend, my worst enemy. i'm not okay when we're apart but i pretend to be." he sung pulling me closer and kissed on my neck.

"i threw the part of the century and people came over no one left sober. and it was all for you, it was all for youuu." we sung to each other and i laughed while he peppered my face with kisses.

"let's go to the car..." he whispered pulling me towards the exit.

"azaire-"

"pleaseee ma." he whined.

i just followed him to his car and watched as he unlocked the door before getting in the back pulling me on top of him.

i straddled his waist once he locked the doors and his hands immediately went underneath my skirt gripping my ass.

i leaned forward pressing my lips against his, the kiss quickly turned sloppy. i turned his head to the side and left a few marks on his neck and i could feel his boner pressing against my clit.

i slowly rocked my hips against him and he groaned gripping my neck making me face him again.

"i love you so much ma..." he rasped as i undid his pants.

"i love you more baby..." i said looking into his eyes, he pulled my underwear down then i felt him slowly slide me down onto his length.

i moaned loudly as he stretched me out, he scooted up and wrapped my legs around him,"hold onto me.." he said before thrusting into me.

his hand tightly gripped my neck while he fucked me from underneath at a fast pace,"shit...you so fuckin wet ma....this pussy mines?" he asked and i nodded whining as soon as he sent a hard smack to my ass.

"i asked you a question pretty." he said making me look into his eyes.

"y-yesss it's yours azaire..." i whined as he rubbed my clit at a fast pace.

his strokes never slowed down as i came on him,"mhmm...keep cumming fa me.." he rasped and i felt myself squirt as my legs shook.

i felt him nut inside me but that didn't stop him as he carefully flipped me onto the seat on my back and continued drilling my shit.

"azaire! fuck baby wait.." i whined as he slowed down stroking deep inside me looking down at where we connected.

his hands gripping my thighs making me take all of him at once,"hm? wassup ma." he said looking in my eyes.

i grabbed his face pulling him into a kiss and he moaned in my mouth before cumming inside me again,"man shit...i should've never took that damn honey." he grumbled pulling out.

he was STILL hard.

"we can go back to the house..." i suggested and he smirked before sliding back into me making me moan loudly.

"we definitely doing more rounds in the room..." he said before kissing my lips and slowly started stroking me all over again.

# Chapter 30

♥

A zaire kade carmine

i groaned as i slowly woke up my head was throbbing and my mouth felt dry as fuck.

i took in my surroundings, i realized my head was laying on xylah chest and she was asleep beside me.

i lifted up the covers and saw we were both naked, i noticed the love marks on her neck and chest and smiled.

last night i was going crazy, i already know she gonna complain about soreness.

i reached for my phone and went to my camera roll for last night, yeah we was definitely gone.

my eyes widened at a video from last night, it was on the nightstand and started with me eating xylah out and ended with her riding me.

so much was done inbetween the video being long as hell so i was skipping thru it,"damn...we needa be pornstars." i mumbled as she moved around.

"ma..." i rasped kissing all over her face and she whined.

"babyy...sleep." she mumbled moving closer to me.

"get uppp...you needa feed my son." i said and she huffed sitting up holding the cover against her.

"what we gonna eat?" she asked and i shrugged.

"you wanna see if the gang wanna try and find an ihop or sumn?" i asked and she nodded.

"how you feeling?" she asked.

"honestly i gotta headache...but i feel great like from the room to the club last night, i ain't felt this happy in a minute ma." i said truthfully and she smiled.

"im glad i've made it fun so far." she said and i nodded kissing her lips.

"more than that, you helping me take my mind off that shit at home." i said and she nodded scratching her acrylics against my durag.

the shit felt good as fuck whenever she did it, i usually hated people touching my head and shit but i loved when she did it.

"speaking of...i'm willing to move into the house with you before azriel gets here. that way we don't have to worry about a newborn and moving into the house at the same time." she said and i smiled hard as fuck.

"i'm so glad...i've already started ordering furniture but it's the stuff you be looking at i ordered. we can look at other stuff together and order the rest." i said and she nodded pecking my lips.

"i'll like that baby, and what kinda nursery you wanna do for him?" she asked and i thought.

"let's do toy story." i suggested and she nodded.

"okay, when we go home we can look at different stuff for that." she said it was a knock on the door and i pulled the cover over us more,"yooo!" i yelled and benz walked in wit ayani behind him.

"damnn y'all still in bed? y'all must've been fuckin like rabbits." benz said and ayani smacked his chest.

"hush, y'all got 20 minutes max. we hungry and want ihop." ayani said.

"damn azaire, xylah tore yo neck up." benz cackled and i quickly looked into the camera on my phone.

"and i thought i did you dirty..." i mumbled seeing the multiple hickeys on my neck and they weren't small either.

they left out our room and i helped xylah with everything since she was either limping or sumn hurt when she stretched too much.

"you not getting no more pussy for rest of this weekend." she said and i clutched my chest.

"what?" i asked craning my neck and she busted out laughing.

"it ain't that good—"

"yes it is, yo pussy got crack in it bae." i frowned and she shook her head.

"get dressed azaire." she said zipping up the front of her bodysuit then buttoned up her jeans.

her hair was clipped back and she was going natural with no make up or lashes, she looked good as hell.

now we were at the beach, xylah in between my legs leaning against me as she ate her strawberries she dipped in sugar.

taylin and sage were in the water, while benz and ayani dug in the sand making sandcastles.

"you want one?" xylah asked handing me a strawberry and i took it taking a bite.

"yo son kicking me." she mumbled grabbing my hand and put it on her lower abdomen.

almost immediately i felt about 3 kicks back to back,"damn he active." i laughed.

"yes he been beating my ass ever since we ate breakfast." she said with a pout.

"he just letting you know he ready for whatever." i said kissing her cheek.

i finished the strawberry she gave me then got up helping her up as well,"water time." she said grabbing my hand and i followed behind her watching her ass jiggle.

she had on swim shorts that hugged her butt and a small bikini top.

"you look so pretty ma." i said kissing her forehead then her lips.

"thank you baby, you look so handsome...especially with all yo tattoos on display." she said running her acrylics over my chest and stomach.

"say i won't fuck you in this water?" i said squinting my eyes at her.

"hornball move." she laughed walking until the water was at her waist.

i stood close by her holding her waist before picking her up,"bae i know i'm heavy by now." she said handing onto me.

"nah, i like holding you. ain't nun gonna stop me from doing that." i said pecking her lips multiple times.

"mmm..i can tell." she said staring hard at me and started playing with my earlobes.

"you think we should get his ears pierced while he a baby?" she asked and i shrugged.

"i mean why not...hell i did it." i said and she nodded.

"okay i was just wondering what you thought about it cause everybody has different opinions." she said rubbing over my beard hairs.

"i'm cool with doing it, i wanna hold him while he get them pierced tho." i said and she laughed.

"okay baby you can do that." she said and i walked back to shore with her in my arms before putting her down.

i reached down in the bag we bought and handed her a water bottle which she happily took to drink.

i stared at her as she downed half the bottle and grabbed her phone,"later yall going go karting while me and the girls to the spa, then y'all going to spa while we'll be at the house. when y'all done we going out to eat." she said.

"ight...if i get first place i can eat yo pussy?" i asked and she shook her head.

"you finna take a tolerance break from that." she said patting my shoulder and i mugged.

"yeah okay, don't play wit me xylah." i said as she laughed.

"i'm not laughing...i'm not.." i mumbled rubbing her stomach and felt azriel kicking.

i leaned down and kissed her stomach a few times,"hey babyboy i can't wait for you to get here, we gonna be jumping yo mama."

"azaire." xylah said glaring at me and i laughed standing back up.

# Chapter 31

♥

Xylah turned off the light to azriel's closet, she had just finished organizing the baby products nalani bought for them to use.

she waddled over to the bedroom her and azaire shared, azaire had fallen asleep with his computer open most his clothes still on.

xylah walked over to him pecking his lips then closed his computer and placed it on charge for him.

a contraction hit her and she groaned rubbing her stomach, she was 38 weeks pregnant and the midwife already warned her baby boy would probably come before the 40 weeks were up.

she went to the bathroom and stripped from azaire's t-shirt then turned the water all the way to hot.

she took around 15 minutes to shower then got out wrapping a robe around her body, right as she brushed her teeth she felt her water break.

she groaned again as another contraction hit her hard, she snatched off her shower cap but kept on bonnet that was on her braids.

"mmm...okay baby boy, hollon let's get daddy up.." she mumbled rubbing her stomach and waddled back into the bedroom.

"azaire!" she semi-yelled and his eyes slowly opened.

"hmm??" he hummed trying to close his eyes back.

"mmcht- azaireee." she whined as another contraction hit her.

"what's wrong ma?" he asked yawning.

she grabbed the closest thing to her which was baby wipes before throwing them at him making him jump up,"bruh why the fuck-"

"my water broke!"

azaire quickly moved from the bed going to the closet,"xylah—where the baby bag?" he asked with wide eyes.

"i don't knowwww." she groaned rubbing her stomach.

"shit man- how far apart are your contractions?"

"azaire! stop asking me stupid shit and let's just goooo!"

"okay okay! hollon look breathe fa me, i gotta get our bags to the car..." he said grabbing the keys, he went to pick her up until she pushed him back.

"i got it- move." she grumbled waddling past him.

"ma, i'm not finna argue come on." he said quickly picking her up bridal style and made his way to the front door.

"how you feeling?" matiyah asked xylah.

xylah shrugged as she ate crushed ice, soon as she got to the hospital she quickly asked for the epidural and she was 4 cm dilated.

azaire sat on the bed beside xylah allowing her to play with his fingers to help calm her nerves,"azaire..."

"yes ma?"

"no more kids." she mumbled and he shook his head.

"yeah okay ma." he said before kissing her cheek.

"you don't want no more foreal?" she asked wit a frown.

"you just said-"

"shut up." she cut him off and he nodding shutting up.

"yeah she just like yo ass..." namari mumbled to matiyah.

"hush up." matiyah said mushing namari's head.

"heyyy my familyyy, how you feeling?" nalani asked walking in the room wit scrubs on.

"good...how much longer?" xylah asked and nalani shrugged.

"that's up to him, you've been drinking the tea i gave you?" xylah nodded to nalani's question.

"then you should be good, plus you have the epidural you shouldn't feel anything." nalani said.

"your fine wit me checking how dilated you are?" nalani asked and xylah nodded.

she rather somebody she knew and had the education to do it rather then a nurse she didn't know.

"damn you dilated quick as fuck— y'all ain't hear me cuss. umm you at 7cm now. 3 more cm and he'll be on the way...try walking around some or bouncing on the yoga ball." nalani suggested then checked her contractions and the baby's heart rate.

xylah forced herself up,"look we're gonna be outside okay? if you need us tell azaire to get us." matiyah said before kissing xylah's forehead.

xylah watched them walk out then looked over at azaire before bursting into tears.

azaire quickly got up pulling xylah into a hug,"what's wrong ma? talk to me baby." he said as she hugged him back tightly.

"i'm scared...i don't know what if i can't push him out? what if sumn goes wrong? what if i can't love him properly azaire?!" she spoke through sobs as he rubbed her back.

"shhhh...your gonna be the best mama out here baby. i promise you, imma be here wit you every step of the way. your not doing this alone you got me and your family and the gang. you know we always gonna be here for you." he said kissing her nose.

her sobs soon calmed down as she held onto azaire who slowly rocked them side to side,"thank you..." xylah mumbled into azaire's chest.

"you don't-"

"no not jus for this...but everything seriously. before you i really didn't do much or go outside, you introduced me to different things and i'm glad you did. you've stayed by my side and went all out for me when you never had to." she said staring up at him.

azaire felt his cheeks heat up and cleared his throat before speaking,"because ma...yo ass deserve the world and i mean that shit. we all need someone to stay."

"you've showed me love in different ways and showed me it's not just about what i can get you, but what i actually do fa you and what you do fa me...i don't be ever wanna lose you xylah. i wanna marry you, grow old with you, build a family with you and only you." he said staring right back at her.

"i love you." xylah said feeling her eyes get watery.

"i love you more...don't cry ma." he said wiping her eyes then connected their lips.

xylah pulled back once she heard a knock on the door,"aye- cut allat that's why she finna push a baby out now." benz said walking in first then ayani mushed his head.

the rest of the gang walked in while xylah went to sit on the bed,"leave them alone, how you feeling?" sage asked walking over to the bed.

"good...ready for him to get here." xylah said and they all went into different conversations until it was time for xylah to push.

xylah stood over the bassinet with azaire beside her, inside the bassinet was azriel's small body. it took 30 minutes of pushing for him to enter the world.

he screamed loudly until he was laid on xylah's chest, he instantly calmed down and looked around the room with wide eyes.

his eyes actually landed on azaire first then xylah, he weighted 5 pounds and 7 ounces.

"he so adorable..." xylah cooed and azaire nodded his head agreeing.

"he look like you ma." azaire said and xylah laughed.

"you saying i look like an alien?"

"not too much on him, give him more time to marinate. but i can tell he's gonna look like you." azaire said kissing her cheek.

"y'all got the same nose." azaire said and xylah smiled.

"i guess.." she said and carefully picked azriel from the bassinet and held him to her chest.

she got back in the hospital bed, azaire sat beside her just staring at the both of them in awe.

azaire grabbed the small cap for azriel's head and placed it on him,"i'm surprised you never had heartburn."

"me too, my mama had it wit me and the twins..." xylah said as azriel's eyes started opening.

"i think he hear us talking about him." xylah said and azriel moved his head towards her voice.

"boy put that head down, too early for allat." azaire said as xylah placed her hand behind azriel's head.

# Chapter 32

♥

Few months later...

azaire kade carmine

"ganggg what you doing today?" taylin asked as i answered the group facetime.

"going home to my family." i said starting my car and started my drive to chic fil a.

"dayummm needa bring nephew over here." taylin said and i laughed.

"i'll talk to xylah, she might let y'all stop by today." i said.

"she need to, miss y'all dumbasses." benz said.

"benz shut the hell up being loud bruh damn." i heard ayani's voice in the background.

"bit— ight nigga." benz mumbled and i laughed.

"what's it like being a dad though??" taylin asked.

"personally i love it, he definitely a mamas boy but he'll cuddle with me every now and then. or if i gotta bottle for him." i said and they laughed.

"but nah i'm glad to be a dad foreal and it makes me go harder you know? cause not only do i got xylah but i gotta son too." i said.

"damn his ass making me wanna quit the streets and have a lil family." benz mumbled.

"yeah take yo time on the family part, but i've been thinking about leaving...i know one day sage gonna want to have kids...and the last thing i wanna do is fuck around and die while she having my kid." taylin said.

"ayani- you ever gonna want kids?" benz asked her and i heard ayani smack her lips.

"benz you gonna piss me offff, you know i'm tryna nap."

"lemme fuck sumn." he said and i saw a pillow hit his face.

"i'll call y'all back." benz said before hanging up.

i held the bags full of food as i unlocked the door before locking it back, i could hear azriel babbling from the kitchen.

i walked in to the kitchen and saw xylah holding him while she washed out his bottles.

"pretty girl." i called out and watched her turn around and smile.

"hey baby." she said walking over to me and kissed me.

she had on a black sports bra with black shorts, her knotless braids up in a messy bun.

"you look sexy as hell..." i said kissing her again and she pulled back.

"yo son right here chill." she said and i kissed azriel's cheek making him squeal and reach for me.

i gladly took him from her arms then placed the chic fil a bag on the counter, "that's for you ma, you can chill i'll clean the rest." i said and she nodded.

"okay thank you- also the girls mentioned coming over today."

"so did the boys, i just wanted to see how you were feeling first." i said and she nodded.

"they can come, i've missed them a lil." she said grabbing the food.

i watched as she sat at the kitchen island and started eating then i looked at azriel who was already staring at me.

"wassup man? you and yo mama been having fun?" i talked to him and he babbled back whenever he seen fit.

i held him in one arm and rinsed all the suds off the bottles with my other hand.

"baby, in a few hours we're going out to eat and everyone gonna meet us at the restaurant." she said and i nodded.

"how you think he gonna act??" i asked and she shrugged.

"i don't know...imma bring extra milk and his toys so maybe he won't show out too much." she said.

"plus knowing him he'll fall asleep fast as hell." i said and she laughed.

"oh he definitely gonna get his sleep he don't care what going on." she said shaking her head.

which was true this boy has slept through, thunderstorms, vacuums, and loud ass music.

azriel started whining and rubbing his eyes," speaking of sleep...imma put him to sleep real quick then dry the bottles." i said and she gave me a thumbs up as she stuffed fries into her mouth.

xylah was probably one of the only girls i knew who would change their hair constantly and fast as hell too.

before leaving the house she managed to take down her braids then put on a bob wig, and make it look good as fuck.

"i'm not gonna hold you...i wanna get you pregnant again." i told her and she laughed from the backseat.

"can our soon enjoy a lil more time being the only child." she said and i looked at her through the rear view mirror.

she was currently feeding him a bottle as i drove to the restaurant.

"he got 9 months..." i mumbled.

"tell yo daddy, no more siblings for a while." she cooed to him.

i finally made it and parked near the front, i let her finish feeding him while i got on my phone scrolling through insta then landed on her story.

i liked her story and swiped up with heart eyes and 'my fine ass wife'.

"really azaire? i'm in the car wit you." she laughed and i shrugged getting out.

"i don't care, you know imma foreva hype yo beautiful ass up." i said opening the back door.

azriel eyes looked towards me and he gave me a gummy smile making me smile,"wassup, you ready to meet yo aunts and uncles?"

"send me that picture you posted too." i told xylah and she nodded grabbing his bag while i got him out his car seat.

we walked into the restaurant hand in hand,"aye! over here!"

"only benz ghetto ass." xylah said shaking her head.

i sat by taylin and xylah was beside me on the outside,"do you guys need a high chair?" a waiter asked and xylah nodded her head.

"oh my goshhh he's so cute." sage gushed as azriel looked around at everyone.

"he look like xylah but definitely got azaire's lips." ayani said.

"yeah them definitely yo fat ass lips." benz said.

"not too much on they lips." xylah said grabbing azriel and placed him in the high chair.

azriel whined at first until xylah gave him a straw from the table to play with.

i shook my head then quickly got on my phone to post the picture xylah sent me.

my story 30s

send a message

"dayummm my friend pressureee." ayani said and xylah laughed some.

"and she snapped back after having a babyy- yeah yo favs could never." ayani joined in.

"i'm starting to think you a lil gay." benz said to ayani.

"bet i could fuck yo sister too." ayani said and benz mugged her.

"y'all sick." xylah said shaking her head.

"can i get y'all started on drinks??"

we all told the waiter our drinks before he left,"girl i know you happy you can finally drink again." ayani said and xylah nodded.

"yeahh that's why i pump extra milk so i don't have to worry about it being in my system." she said looking at azriel who was in his own world looking around at everything.

"first night she came home...faced a whole backwood by herself." i said and xylah laughed.

"and diddd, labor was exhausting...i'd probably do it again tho."

"so you saying you pregnant?" sage asked.

"oh fuck no." xylah and i said in sync.

"y'all said that a lil too fast, azaire know he want more kids." taylin said and i nodded.

"i do...but imma let him get older first." i said and azriel started whining making xylah pick him up.

he started whining again reaching for me and i took him into my arms, his head instantly went against my chest.

"i thought you said he was a mamas boy?" taylin asked.

"it's probably cause i've been at work all day..." i mumbled patting azriel's back.

# Chapter 33

♥

Xylah sailor summer

"mommy...my ipad dead." azriel said and i stalefaced him before sighing.

"go tell yo daddy to find yo charger..." i said as i changed the twins diapers.

"yes ma'am!" he quickly said before running off.

i sighed looking at the twins,"y'all always wanna do stuff in sync ..damnnn." i said before gagging.

they both had blow outs,"mama!!" london babbled as i wiped her butt then placed a new diaper on her.

"now go run." i said sitting her down on the ground then did the same with landon.

i put him down and he immediately ran around with london making me laugh.

i groaned rubbing my stomach as i felt the baby kick.

"xylah-"

"what!" i snapped looking back at azaire.

"uh...nevermind..." he mumbled.

"nooo bae i'm sorry." i quickly said and he walked over to me kissing my forehead.

"i told you i was gonna get the twins ready ma, go relax." he said and i pouted.

"but i feel like i don't help much! and-"

"ma...you done gave me 3 kids finna be 4. trust me you've done a lot and you stay home with them when they're not in daycare...it's fine baby sit down and relax until we have to leave." he said then pecked my lips a few times.

"okay..." i mumbled and he smiled down at me.

"you so pretty baby...i'm happy as fuck you finna be my wife." he said grabbing my hand that had my engagement ring on it.

"me too, i'm glad we ended up together foreal.." i said and he kissed my lips then leaned down to kiss my stomach.

"lil nigga stop kicking my lips." he said and i laughed .

"leave him alone." i said and he shrugged.

"alright- landon ! london! come on so y'all can get dressed!" he yelled and they both quickly ran into the room.

"waittt sit them both in the front so i can take their pictures." i told azaire and he did as i said.

i felt azriel hug my legs making me look down at him,"hollon imma pick you up in a minute." i told him and he nodded.

i snapped the pictures of the twins and smiled when i finally had the one i wanted.

"landon can never look towards the camera." i heard making me turn and see my brothers.

"damnnn xylah you pregnant again?" jamari asked looking at my stomach.

"you just don't know how to pull out huh?" kamari asked azaire as he picked up azriel.

azaire thumped kamari's forehead,"shut the fuck up." he bucked at him.

"yeah shut the fuck up." azriel repeated and i glared at him.

"sorry mommy." he quickly said and i shook my head.

"whew! after this i'm getting my tubes tied..." i mumbled as jamari grabbed landon and azaire grabbed london.

we walked towards my parents house me knocking on the door,"wassup— oh my gawdddd againnnn?!" namari asked looking at my stomach.

my mama quickly pushed her out the way,"oh my goshhh i knew i dreamed about fishes for a reason! its xylah!" my mama said grabbing my hand and pulled me inside where everyone else was.

"hey nieceyy, you know what you having?" aunt nalani asked as she hugged me.

"another boy...london gonna be the only girl." i pouted and she laughed.

"that's if y'all don't have no more."

"we not." azaire and i quickly said in sync.

"get y'all crotch goblins." namari said as the twins ran towards her.

i laughed watching namari run around the couch the twins right behind her,"gg!!" azriel said running to my grandma.

"told you he like me more." grandma said picking azriel up and stuck her tongue out at granny.

"fuck up tahani..." granny said before coming over to hug me.

"don't worry you still my favorite." i told granny and she rolled her eyes.

"i don't wanna hear that…plus this new baby on the way? oh i'm not watching i'm so serious." she said and i eyed her.

"you said that wit the last three." azaire said and granny waved him off.

"you worry about pulling out next time-"

"y'all ever think maybe it be her? why i gotta be responsible for pulling out." he said wit a frown and i laughed.

the last two times i got pregnant was actually from me not moving when he said he was about to…but in my defense.

a bitch dickmatized a lil…okay A LOT!

"anywaysss." i said and we changed the subject.

"sooo how all the wedding stuff coming along?" mama asked while i rubbed my stomach.

"mmm good, we mostly got everything together i'm just wanting to have this baby before i get measured for my dress i already know what kind i want." i said then heard a bag of chips open.

i looked over and azriel was on the floor with a bag of ruffles he got from my brothers.

"that's good…" my mama said then kissed my forehead before attending to the twins who were torturing namari.

"you don't need no more of them after this one." namari said sounding out of breath.

i nodded agreeing, i wasn't even supposed to be having this one…when they say you're more fertile after pregnancy.

BELIEVE EM!

azriel is 4, the twins about to be 1 and now i'm 6 months pregnant. 0/10 recommend.

but at the end of the day, i truly love my babies and they keep my entertained and motivated.

i graduated high school and also took some college courses just in case i did decide one day i didn't want to permanently be a stay at home wife.

but right now it was definitely looking like stay at home wife.

"xylah!" jamari called me and i looked over at him and kamari.

they waved me towards the kitchen and i slowly got up with the help of azaire before following them.

"wassup??" i asked and kamari looked nervous as hell.

"you know how our parents were like invite who we want over?" jamari asked and i nodded.

"well...only i know but kamari's gay- but he never told y'all and he's scared for his boyfriend to come." jamari said and i looked over at kamari.

"really???" i asked and kamari shrugged looking down.

"c'mere." i said holding my arms out.

kamari walked into my arms and i hugged him tightly,"you don't have to be scared kay...one our parents are gay, two uncle rome and uncle leo?? boy nobody is gonna get mad at you or upset. you know we all love you to death." i said.

"i know...i'm just i don't know nervous i guess." he said and i nodded.

"that's understandable but it's gonna be fine really- lemme guess yo player ass ain't invite nobody." i said to jamari.

"actually...mama and mom probably finna have a heart attack..." he said scratching his neck.

"what???" i asked.

"JAMARI CAMERON SUMMER!!!" mama yelled making all our eyes go wide.

she barely yells— and especially not our full names.

kamari forced jamari out first and i followed pursuit.

my jaw slightly dropping seeing a girl looking like she was ready to pop at any minute,"sumn you wanna tell me?" mama asked glaring at jamari.

"umm...xylah not the only one finna have a baby??" he said and i popped his lip.

"unt unt i'm damn near married and grown don't add me in nan." i said going to my seat and kamari followed me.

"it must be a coldddd day in hell..." namari said rubbing her temple.

# *Epilogue*

♥

"Unt unt...you sure you not pregnant again??" ayani asked as xylah threw up for the third time this morning.

"it's just nerves...and i haven't ate." xylah said as she leaned over the toliet.

"well...i ain't tryna rush but...we gotta finish your makeup and still get your hair situated..." sage said as she held xylah's bundles back.

"i know i know just—" xylah stopped talking as more vomit came up.

sage and ayani made eye contact with each other before speaking,"she pregnant again."

"stoppp." xylah whined before finally getting up.

she brushed her teeth yet again as matiyah came in with saltine crackers and ginger ale,"hmm this should help you until the reception."

xylah ate the crackers while matiyah quickly ran the flat iron through her bundles, the hair came down to xylah's ass.

it was a side part with dramatic edges, sumn she wouldn't keep in long just for the special occasion such as her wedding.

a million thoughts were running through her head but one stayed in her head.

'am i pregnant again?'

she shrugged it off as she took a few sips of ginger ale then allowed the hired makeup artists to finally start on her face.

"whewww this dress is bombbb." nalani dragged as she fluffed out the bottom of the dress with sage's help.

"lord i don't even wanna talk about how much that shit costed." namari spoke and nalani nudged her.

"shut up, it was yo ass who told her go all out anyway." nalani said and namari shrugged.

"you right...my baby girl deserve everything, this wedding definitely cost a arm and a damn liver but i'd give her the whole world if she asked." namari spoke truthfully before sniffling.

"bae i know you not finna cry." matiyah said and namari waved her off.

"all these years...and you still look at her as your own, like she still a baby or sumn." nalani said putting her arm around namari.

"shut up bitch." namari said before walking to xylah.

xylah stared up at namari and namari stared back,"you pregnant again?"

xylah groaned,"nooo i wish y'all would stop saying that."

"mhmm...we'll see. you ready tho? like for me to walk you down the isle. we gonna play set it off." namari said with a smirk and xylah laughed.

"nah we can play that at the reception tho." xylah said smiling at namari.

"and no twerking at the reception either." namari said.

xylah and matiyah both smacked their lips before laughing,"you better be gone be 7 o'clock then cause 7:01...twerking till my knees give out!" xylah said as sage high-fived her.

"clock it!" ayani yelled fixing london's dress.

"yeah okay...ya nasties. matiyah you know damn well you ain't shaking ass." namari said.

"girl i'm grown as fuck! don't worry i'll throw it back on you only baby." matiyah said and xylah gagged.

"i think y'all forgot i was throwing up not too long ago..." she mumbled and they all laughed.

azaire sat in the room with his groomsmen staring down at the ground, he was excited about getting married beyond that but one thing was missing.

his mother.

he hated his mother just turned weird once xylah got pregnant with azriel, not once did she see any of her grandkids and it definitely fucked with his head.

especially when his mom and dad was all he knew, now he only had his dad who was currently in the room.

"you okay son?"

"hmm..yeah i'm cooling it's just.. i don't know i can't even have that mother son dance. i shouldn't care but it's hard..." he mumbled and aaron rubbed his sons back.

"i know...look don't let that fuck up yo mood, in a few minutes you gonna be able to watch your bride walk down the isle to you."

azaire quickly smiled at the thought, all his worries going away as he thought about seeing and holding xylah again.

"yeah...you right..." he said before getting up.

"niggaaaa what dances we doing at the reception? cause i'm tryna be fucked up when i get back to the hotel..." benz asked and azaire laughed.

"any and everything...and we definitely mixing drinks tonight fuck it." azaire said.

"i know that's right! on god i'm finna get sage pregnant tonight." taylin said shaking his head.

"sick as fuck..i ain't going that damn far." benz said shaking his head.

"whattt? i'm tryna catch up wit xylah and azaire! you and ayani already gotta baby." taylin said which was true.

benz and ayani had a 2 year old daughter, she was definitely the quiet one out of everybody but she loved her parents deeply.

"yeah yeah anywaysss." benz said.

"aye...you know they said xylah been throwing up all morning..." benz said and azaire eyes widened.

"nigga what?"

"ahhhh hell- don't tell me y'all got another on the way." taylin said and azaire's eyes looked over at his youngest son, ayden who was going on 2

"dear god...we don't need anymore but if she is...gonna have to suck that shit up." azaire said rubbing his hand over his face.

my pocket's definitely gonna be empty then... he thought to himself

"nigga at this point start using protection...clear you don't like pulling out." benz said shaking his head.

"and don't the fuck." azaire said making them buss out laughing.

it was after the wedding so everyone's emotions were starting to go down from the emotional ceremony.

"i ain't think you was gonna cry baby..." xylah said as she played with azaire's fingers.

"you my wife now...that shit insane to me and you so fuckin beautiful ma." he said before pecking her glossed lips.

azaire finished smoking his blunt before putting it out, his eyes slightly low and red.

"you sure you don't wanna smoke bae??" azaire asked and xylah shook her head.

"i'm good, i'm tryna drink really." she said then glanced over at the pregnancy test that was loading.

"that's if that bitch don't say pregnant." azaire said shaking his head.

"i know- i'm praying so damn bad...we gotta stop fuckin." xylah said and azaire raised his eyebrows.

"yeah definitely not.." he said watching xylah change from her wedding dress to the reception dress.

"you think this too much??" xylah asked as she fixed the top of the dress to fit her boobs, that were lowkey spilling at the top.

"hell nah...if you ain't pregnant you'll be by the end of the night..." azaire said standing up and grabbed her waist.

"azaire!" she laughed lightly hitting his chest.

"what? i'm kidding...maybe.." he mumbled the last part before kissing her.

she kissed back wrapping her arms around his neck, they pulled back hearing her phone alarm go off.

she quickly turned it off and azaire picked up the test before cheering and picking xylah up,"what! what!" xylah quickly asked.

"we ain't having no mo kids!" he said making her laugh.

"yesss so i can drink, this calls for another blunt actually." xylah said and azaire laughed.

"i gotchu after everybody do they speeches ma." he said sitting down and made her straddle his lap.

"you remember our handshake??" he randomly asked and xylah thought before nodding.

they did their handshake they made in the very beginning with huge smiles on both of their faces.

"baby...." xylah started and azaire hummed staring at her with low eyes.

"i love you so much..." she said.

"i love you so much more...i swear ain't nun ever gonna happen to us." he said before it was a knock on the door.

"hurry up! better not be making no mo babies!" benz yelled from behind the door making them laugh.

"we coming nigga!" azaire yelled back before standing up with xylah in his arms.

everyone else has already made their entrance and now it was time for mr and mrs to make theirs.

"azaire before we go...i know your upset your mom didn't come sooo my mama gonna do the mother son dance wit you." xylah said and azaire eyes widened.

"w-what?" he slightly stuttered and xylah shook her head.

"i ain't hear that in a minute." she said and azaire cleared his throat.

"she is?" he asked and xylah nodded.

"damn....yo family really the best..." azaire said as they walked out.

"we know bookie." aspen said making tahani grab her hand and lead them to their seats.